THIS BOOK MUST BE RE
ON OR BEFORE THE LAS

VISIT OUR WEBSITE ww
(Borrower and PIN number required for this service)

ISLE OF WIGHT LIBRARIES

DONATION

Ve   6/21

First edition, published in colour in 2021 by FeedARead.com

Copyright © text and illustrations Elizabeth Morley 2021

The author has asserted her moral right under the
Copyright, Designs and Patents Act, 1988, to be identified
as the author of this work.

A CIP catalogue record for this title is available from the British
Library.

For M

It was late October. A gale was blowing across the Isle of Needles, turning the grey sea white in a confusion of waves. Most hedgehogs who could took refuge indoors. As for Hoglinda, she barely noticed. The home she shared with her father lay in a sheltered spot, nestling at the foot of the downs and half surrounded by trees. Though the house overlooked Brambling Harbour, it lay some two miles from the open sea.

Hoglinda's father, Admiral Hoglander, had already set off on his morning walk. Being a creature of habit, he always followed the same route - up onto the downs and then along the high cliff tops. From there he would watch the ships through his spyglass and amuse himself by guessing what cargo they carried and where they were sailing to. But Hoglinda was tired of doing the same old walk day after day and had chosen to stay at home. Unfortunately, her cousin Quiller, who was staying with them, was out at the local shipyard on business. So she would have to entertain herself. First she played a few pieces of music on her harpsichord. Then she read a little. When she had had enough of reading, she pawed over her folder of drawings and paintings, wondering whether there were any views nearby that she

had not already attempted. Unable to think of any, she put down the folder and, stifling a yawn, began to pace up and down the room.

It was raining now. She paused to gaze through the rain-streaked window, reflecting on what a lucky escape she had had. It was then that she noticed the tree tops swaying in the wind. They hardly ever swayed like that, and it would be a great deal windier on the cliff tops. Her thoughts were cast back to a storm the previous winter: a hedgehog had fallen to his death from those cliffs. Suddenly afraid, she grabbed her cloak, scribbled a message for her cousin and set off in pursuit of her father.

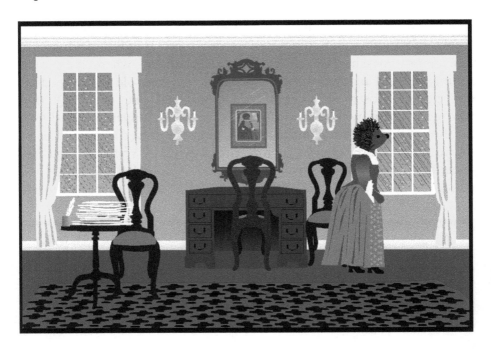

As she climbed the steep slope behind the house, Hoglinda noticed that Brambling Harbour was much rougher than usual; at the top, hit by the full force of the wind, she struggled to keep upright. But she had spotted her father. She shouted. But he could not hear above the wind and it was no use waving, as he was turned the other way, so she pressed on and caught up with him as quickly as she could.

"Papa!" she said breathlessly, as she came up behind him.

Admiral Hoglander turned round and smiled with puzzled pleasure. "Hoglinda! What on earth brings you out in this weather?" His smile turned into a frown. "Is something wrong? Has something happened?"

6

"No, papa, nothing has happened - except that I was worried about you - that is all."

"Tush!" said the admiral. "I have weathered many a worse storm than this at sea."

"But you are not at sea now. Come, let us go home before the weather gets any worse."

The admiral glanced up at the sky. There were two layers of dark cloud moving in different directions. It suggested that worse weather was, indeed, on the way.

"Very well, my dear, I - "

The admiral broke off before he had finished his sentence, for he had just then noticed a ship. Her sails were close-hauled and she was trying to head away from the land; but wind and tide were sweeping her relentlessly on.

"Oh!" exclaimed Hoglinda, who had followed her father's gaze. "That ship is far too close to the shore, is she not?"

"Indeed she is," said the admiral grimly. He got out his spyglass to take a closer look. "Well I never! She is flying the colours of my old enemy!"

The admiral was referring to the Furzish Navy. Great Bristlin and Furze had, in fact, been at peace for some years now, but it was unclear how long this could last.

"How many hedgehogs can you see on board?" asked Hoglinda.

"I count seventeen on deck," said the admiral. "For a cutter of that size, that may well be the entire crew."

For a moment he wondered where the cutter was bound for and for what purpose. Great Bristlin was currently fighting to put down a rebellion in its western colonies, and the Furzish Navy was known to be sending guns to those very same rebels. In an attempt to stop this, the Bristlish Navy had taken to boarding and searching any foreign ships it came across, which was naturally greatly resented by the Furzish. The admiral wondered whether this cutter was also carrying guns to the rebels, but there was no way of telling. And, now that the cutter was in trouble, it no longer mattered. Through his spyglass, he could see that some of the crew had already started to untie the ship's boats and were getting ready to abandon ship. Very soon the cutter had all but disappeared beneath the towering chalk cliffs.

"We must fetch help," said the admiral, without hesitation. No sailor would leave another hedgehog to drown, whoever he might be.

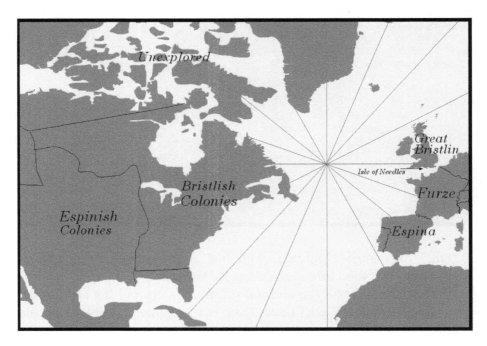

Hoglinda nodded and started to run down to the village, followed closely by her father. Within a half hour, the admiral had set off across the harbour with a little fleet of five fishing boats, rowed by hedgehogs from the village. Hoglinda waited anxiously on the shore, with the local physician and the rescuers' families.

The admiral's crew had to pull hard on their oars as they rowed against the wind. It blew even more strongly when they reached the open sea. Now rowing parallel to the shore among the breaking waves, they were in constant danger of being capsized. Several times they were forced to turn into the waves to save themselves.

Eventually they caught sight of the Furzish cutter. She had been swept onto the rocks. Her boats were adrift, and her crew stood clinging to the deck, with the waves crashing over them. As the admiral's boat came alongside, the swell carried her high above the cutter and the next minute flung her far below. Timing his moment carefully, the admiral threw a line across to the ship-wrecked sailors. They caught and secured it, and the first three climbed across, one by one. Then, with the admiral's little boat full, they turned for home, leaving the next boat to take their place.

Seventeen hedgehogs were saved that day, thanks to the bravery and skill of the islanders. No questions were asked until, some time later, the admiral enquired, as casually as he could, where the Furzish cutter

9

had been sailing to. He was assured that she had simply been patrolling the Furzish coast and been blown off course. The admiral accepted this story. Whether he believed it or not was beside the point - for the cutter and her cargo were now at the bottom of the sea.

The shipwrecked crew were given food and shelter. The admiral himself welcomed two of the survivors into his home: the ship's captain, Lieutenant Oursin, and his one passenger, Monsieur Espinon. They were to stay until such time as their return home could be arranged. The admiral's house, usually so quiet, was suddenly bristling with hedgehogs, since they also had Quiller staying with them - Hoglinda's cousin and nephew of the admiral's late wife.

The five hedgehogs got on well, despite the tension between their two countries, and the time passed pleasantly. Lieutenant Oursin very naturally shared Admiral Hoglander's love of the sea. And Hoglinda soon discovered that Monsieur Espinon shared her love of painting and drawing. Whenever they all went out for walks together, he would ask her to show him the best viewpoints, which of course she was delighted to do. She was also very pleased to be able to speak in Furzish with a native speaker, having only ever spoken the language with her governess until now. But the friendship between Quiller and Espinon was the most striking of all. At first Espinon had seemed to prefer Hoglinda's company. But one day, as they were all out walking

10

around the harbour, something changed. It seemed to Hoglinda almost as though Quiller and Espinon had reached some sort of understanding. From that time onwards, whenever they all went out, Quiller and Espinon would always stride on ahead of the others or drop behind; and, very often, the two of them went out all alone.

Within a few weeks, however, the party had broken up. Quiller returned to his home on the other side of the island; and Lieutenant Oursin found a ship to take his crew and Espinon back to Furze. Life in Brambling returned to normal. The winter passed uneventfully, except that it was colder and wetter than usual, so that Hoglinda longed for spring, when she could paint outside again and her father would take her out in his yacht. But with the arrival of spring came also the arrival of a letter summoning Admiral Hoglander away.

The navy needed the admiral's help with putting down the rebellion in the colonies. These colonies lay far away on the opposite side of the ocean and the voyage there alone would take several weeks. Knowing therefore that he must be away for many months, the admiral was reluctant to leave his young daughter all alone. So he decided to send her to stay with Quiller, as her nearest relative on the island. Quiller was a widower with two young hoglets to bring up, assisted only by his housekeeper and a maid. The admiral felt sure he would welcome the addition of his young cousin to the household.

For her own part, Hoglinda was extremely disappointed. She had hoped to be allowed to join her uncle on the mainland, for he had recently been elected a Member of Parliament and taken his entire family with him to the capital. Hoglinda could imagine few things more exciting than the capital city. But instead she was to be sent to Hog's Edge, a small village in the south-west corner of the Isle of Needles. The area - known locally as 'the Back' of the island - was so remote and wild that, though less than twenty miles from her own home, she had only been there a few times and had never stayed long. Of course, it would be pleasant to get to know little Quillemina and Quillip better; but they were not even near half her age, while Quiller was considerably older than she was. She feared there would be few hedgehogs in the neighbourhood with whom she could have much in common. She imagined the lives they led on the Back to be dull and uneventful. She prepared herself to be bored.

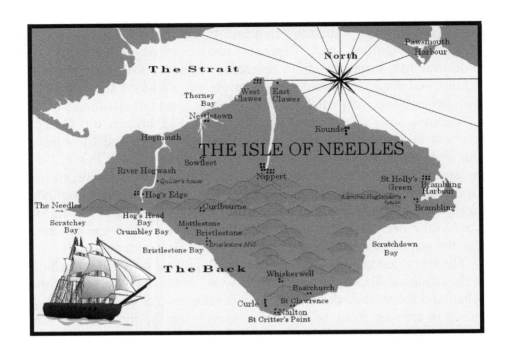

Part One
Chapter One
26th April 1777: half past four in the morning

Hoglinda lay in bed, listening to the wind and the rain. A draught ruffled the fur on her face, and the windows rattled in their frames. But it was another sound altogether that made her prick up her ears. There were voices beneath her window. Quiller had visitors - though it was the middle of the night. Getting up from her bed, she opened the curtains and peered out into the darkness. Three hedgehogs were coming up the path. They clutched lanterns in their paws, but their faces were hidden beneath their hats and a minute later they had disappeared inside. She frowned. Surely no respectable hedgehog would be out and about at this time of night - and on such a night as this!

Yet this had been the way of things ever since Hoglinda had come to live with Quiller, just over a month ago. There had been mysterious comings and goings, sometimes late in the evening but just as often in the middle of the night. Hoglinda had never met any of these nocturnal visitors, Quiller had never spoken to her about them and she had never presumed to ask. Yet she could not help being curious. Quiller lived upon the income from his land: surely there could be no need for him to conduct his business at night!

Unable to suppress her curiosity any longer, she pulled on her dressing gown, lit a candle and crept downstairs. There was light showing under the parlour door. She could hear the crackle of the fire in the hearth and the low murmur of voices. For a moment she considered knocking; but she could think of no reason for interrupting. So, blowing out her candle, she put her ear to the door and listened instead.

Quiller was speaking: "Did you meet anyone tonight, Mr Cutliss?"

"No, sir, that we did not. 'Twas no night for the fainthearted, with the sea so rough and the sky as black as ink."

" 'Twas the same ashore," said a third hedgehog. "We met no one neither. Not that we be done yet and nor is it like we shall be tonight. Problem is, around half the hedgehogs I employ most times, they be ill in bed with the fever - 'tes this accursed cold wind, no doubt. But no matter. The cave'll do well enough for now. We can go back and finish off in the mornen'."

"Hmm," said Cutliss doubtfully. "Let's hope you're right, Mr Tubby. Let's hope you're not caught out by the spring tide."

"Never you worry, Mr Cutliss," said Tubby. "We knows what we be about. The tide won't - " He did not finish his sentence. A floorboard had creaked beneath Hoglinda's feet. "What was that?" he asked. "I thought I heard summat."

Hoglinda stood rooted to the spot - afraid she might be heard if she moved. If only she could just curl up into a ball! For what would she say to Quiller, if he found her eavesdropping at his door? The sound of footsteps behind her startled her into action. She darted into the study just as the housemaid came up from the cellar.

"Oh, it's you, Pinafore!" exclaimed Quiller. He had opened the parlour door and found the maid outside, her paw poised to knock. "We thought we had an intruder."

"Oh, no, sir!" said Pinafore, "that couldn't be - not unless someone climbed in through a window. I locked and bolted the door as soon as my brother left... No, sir, I was just goen' to ask whether you be wanting any more wood for the fire."

"No, we have enough, thank you, Pinafore. You can go back to bed. We shall not want you again tonight."

"Very good, sir. Good night, sir."

Quiller wished her goodnight and shut the parlour door. Hoglinda waited for Pinafore to disappear upstairs, before relighting her candle from the embers of the study fire. She was then about to return upstairs to bed herself, when she noticed that a section of wooden panelling was missing from the wall. It had been removed from beside the fireplace, revealing a narrow windowless chamber beyond. Just visible in the semi-darkness of the chamber was a wooden chest.

Hoglinda stepped inside. The chamber was small from end to end but occupied the full height of the building. With Quiller and his guests next door, she dared not linger long, but it would surely only take a second to look inside the chest. She knelt down and lifted the lid, fully expecting to find something extraordinary inside; but all it contained was a bundle of old clothes, a rather strange glass-bottomed bucket and a leather-bound book.

She opened the book. It was a journal, and the writing was Quiller's - though it was not the journal she had seen him write in. Throughout were numerous references to the times of low and high tide. The letters O and C also appeared frequently – though sometimes the C was written backwards or the O was inked in. She flicked forwards to April the 26th, for it was now the early hours of that day. Here was an inked-in O, followed by the letters HHB; and underneath was written, "High water, four o'clock in the morning": that was barely half an hour ago.

Hoglinda put the journal back in the chest. Then she crept back upstairs, tiptoed past her young cousins' room and closed her own door behind her as quietly as possible. But back in bed she found sleep impossible. Her mind was full of Quiller's secret chamber, his conversation with his late-night visitors, and the journal hidden away in the chest. At first she could make neither head nor tail of it all. Then she remembered that one of the visitors had talked about the sea being rough and the other had mentioned a cave. Perhaps they had brought something ashore and hidden it in the cave. But what and why? Could they be smugglers, she wondered? But no, that was a ridiculous idea! Smugglers were criminals; they brought goods into the country secretly to escape paying the government tax. It was unthinkable that Quiller, her own cousin, would be mixed up with anything like that. He was a respectable hedgehog - the nephew of an admiral!

But then what could it be? Hoglinda was determined to find out. And, when it occurred to her that the HHB in Quiller's journal was very probably Hog's Head Bay, she began to feel she was getting somewhere at last. This was the closest beach to Quiller's house and at one end was a deep cave. Whenever she had been to the bay before, the tide had been far too high for her to get anywhere close to the cave. But one of the visitors - Mr Cutliss - had mentioned there being a spring tide at the moment. That meant greater extremes of both high and low water. So perhaps tomorrow the sea would go out far enough for her to be able to visit the cave on foot.

16

Hoglinda decided to give it a try. She would have to be careful, of course, as Mr Tubby's hedgehogs would be going back at some point. But she had her spyglass with her – it had been a parting gift from her father. So she would be able to look ahead and check there was no one there before proceeding.

As for the tide, she thought it was probably just a matter of timing; and she felt she had all the information she needed to get that right. According to Quiller's journal, high water had been at four o'clock that morning. As the average time between high and low water was about six and a quarter hours, she calculated that low water should be at about a quarter past ten. But it was always safer to arrive while the sea was still retreating. So she would aim to get there a little early. Ten o'clock would do, she decided. Then she immediately fell asleep.

"I hope you were not kept awake by the storm last night," said Quiller, when they sat down to breakfast.

"I was for a while," replied Hoglinda, "and then I thought I heard voices in the parlour." She looked at her cousin to see how he would react. It was the first time that either of them had ever referred to Quiller's night-time visitors, but he seemed untroubled by the question.

"Yes," he said, "I had guests. I had some urgent business to attend to, which could not be put off. I hope you were not much disturbed."

"No, I assure you," replied Hoglinda. "Indeed, I feel quite refreshed this morning. I think I might walk down to the bay after breakfast."

"An excellent idea," said Quiller. "It promises to be a fine day. I'd accompany you myself, if business didn't call me away. But perhaps you could take Quillemina and Quillip with you. Some sea air would do them good after spending the whole of yesterday indoors."

"Why, yes, of course," said Hoglinda, hiding her disappointment. With the two hoglets in tow, she would hardly be free to explore the cave. She tried to think of an excuse for leaving them behind. Then the door opened, and the hoglets themselves appeared. Quillemina rushed

over to her father, with a small circular metallic box clasped in her paw. Quillip, who was the younger of the two, toddled in after his sister, looking delighted with himself.

"Papa, look!" exclaimed Quillemina. "Look what Quip found!" She had never been able to pronounce her brother's name properly, and the name had stuck.

Quiller looked inside the box. "It's a tinderbox," he explained. "These things here, they're for kindling a fire."

"Or lighting a candle," added Hoglinda, helpfully. "Where did you find it, Quip?"

"In de garden."

"Well, it probably belongs to one of your papa's visitors from last night. Don't you think so, Quiller?"

"Possibly. Now, Quip, why don't you put it somewhere safe, until we can discover its owner?"

Quillip looked very serious as he tried to think of somewhere safe. Before he could speak, however, he sneezed several times in quick succession.

"Have you caught a cold?" asked his father.

Quillip nodded. Hoglinda held a paw against his forehead and thought it seemed a little hot. Then, seeing an opportunity, she did the same for Quillemina. "Oh dear, I fear they have *both* caught a cold," she said, frowning. "We had better stay at home after all."

"Oh, you need not abandon your walk," said Quiller, just as she had expected he would. "Pinafore and Mrs Brush will look after the hoglets." Mrs Brush was the housekeeper. Hoglinda breathed a sigh of relief; and, after breakfast, she set off alone.

Quiller's house lay on the eastern bank of the River Hogwash, halfway between the north and south coasts. Following the river as far as the tide mill, Hoglinda crossed over at the causeway. Then she continued through Hog's Edge village, past the church, and on down towards the south coast. By ten o'clock, she was standing on the steep shingle bank of Hog's Head Bay. Just behind her was a marsh; from here the River Hogwash flowed northwards to Hogmouth, providing a convenient waterway connecting the south to the north coast. But to either side of the marsh, the land rose steeply to chalk cliffs. Here and there, the sea had worn away the chalk at its base and, at the far end of the beach, it had created a deep cave.

Hoglinda surveyed the scene. The only vessel moored in the bay at present was Quiller's own ship, the *Hogspur*, which was usually kept on the more sheltered north coast of the island. Hoglinda thought the *Hogspur's* presence in the bay this morning was unlikely to be a coincidence. Pulling out her spyglass, she took a closer look at the cave. The sea was much farther out than on her previous visits. So it looked as though she would indeed be able to reach it on foot now, just as she had hoped. Not being a local, she did not appreciate quite how unusual this was; and, not realizing how variable tide times could be, she failed to notice that the tide was already beginning to turn.

Her only concern at present, in fact, was not to be observed. Looking through her spyglass, she scanned both sea and shore. There were no hedgehogs on board the *Hogspur* that she could see, and the beach was deserted. The only building overlooking the bay was the Hog's Head Inn, and there was no sign of activity there either. She waited a few minutes all the same, in case there was already someone in the cave. Then, finally satisfied that the coast was clear, she pressed on - past the inn, across the shingle and sand beach, and over the rocks scattered all around the headland.

21

As she entered the cave, she was struck by its beauty. The entrance reminded her of the island's grandest churches, with its arches and pillars. A few rays of sunshine penetrated the gloom; and light, reflected from the rock pools, danced on the chalk walls. Beyond that, however, was darkness. She paused, waiting for her eyes to adjust. Gradually the darkness receded. Then she stared, shocked by what she saw.

All along the back of the cave were stacked dozens of small wooden barrels and crates. Though Hoglinda had led a sheltered life, even she knew what this meant. The barrels would contain wine or spirits; while the crates would be packed with dry goods - anything from tea to silk or lace. There could be only one reason for hiding goods such as these at the back of a cave. Her cousin Quiller *was* a smuggler, after all. She had once heard a mainlander claim there was barely a hedgehog on the Isle of Needles who was *not* involved in smuggling, one way or another. Yet she had refused to believe it. After all, neither she nor her father had anything to do with this criminal trade. And even now she found it hard to accept that her own cousin was a smuggler. She was distraught. If he were caught, he would be sent to prison. At best, that meant disgrace and hardship. At worst, it meant death - for prisons were vile, filthy places, rife with disease.

Suddenly anxious to be away, Hoglinda turned round to find, to her horror, there was a rowing boat making directly for the cave. The two hedgehogs on board were almost certainly smugglers - Mr Tubby's hedgehogs returning as promised. She looked round desperately for a place to hide. In the dark recesses of the cave she noticed a split in the rock - just wide enough for a hedgehog to hide in, but narrow and dark enough for her not to be seen. She squeezed into the gap and waited.

Very soon she could hear the splashing of oars as the boat approached. Then there was a thud, more splashing and the sound of scraping, as the boat was pulled up onto the shingle inside the cave.

"Darn it!" exclaimed one of the hedgehogs. "I can't find the list o' customers."

"I has et in my pocket, Ruffley," came the response. "Let me zee... I reckons we should start with Sir Montacute over Mottlestone way. He's ordered a half dozen tubs o' wine but agreed to store a full dozen under hes roof fer the cost of one tub. Then there be Mr Thorneycroft, the Reverend Mr Spillikin, Mr Thistlethwaite and Dr Lancet. They've axed fer a dozen tubs between 'em. The silk and the lace, they be fer Widow Twiglet and Mr Tailor. An' then there's the tea, which es fer

Mrs Furry up at the manor. That's everyone fer now. The rest had theirn last night. So that leaves..." he paused to count. "That leaves another dozen tubs and a couple o' crates to store zomewhere."

"Oh, there should be room enough for a little more at Mr Quiller's," responded his companion. "If not, they can go in the church tower, along wi' the tobacco crates we unloaded last night."

"Right you are. Well, best get started then. They there tubs ain't goen' to shift 'emselves."

As the smugglers continued to chat, their voices echoed around the cave. They seemed frighteningly close. Hoglinda shrank deeper into her hiding place and was surprised to find the narrow space widening out. Stretching out her arms, she was still able to touch both sides. Here and there the walls felt unusually smooth. It suggested the natural split in the rock had been widened artificially to create this passage. She continued along it gingerly, feeling her way as she went and trying not to stumble on the uneven surface. The passage descended a little and then ascended again, before widening out until she could no longer touch both sides.

Stretching her paws out in front of her now, she groped the air. There was something there. A wooden crate and, underneath it, another one. Lifting the lid of the upper crate, she caught the unmistakable aroma of tea. So this inner cave was just another hiding place for the contraband! It was no place for her to be hiding from the smugglers. Yet there was nowhere else for her to go. She crouched down behind the crates and then waited. Only when she was quite certain the smugglers had had plenty of time to fill their boat and be on their way, did she creep back along the passage towards the outer cave.

There were no voices now. She peered out from her hiding place: the barrels were fewer and there was no sign of either the smugglers or their boat. But, as she emerged back into the outer cave, she found herself facing a new danger, for she had miscalculated badly. The tide was already coming in. Indeed, the sea was flooding the cave much faster than she had expected was even possible. Already half the floor had disappeared beneath the rising water.

She waded over towards the cave entrance, hoping it might still be possible to escape; but the sea was now above her knees and getting deeper with every step. Looking out, she was shocked to find the nearest section of beach completely submerged. She dared go no further, for she could not swim. What a fool she had been to come here when she knew nothing of the local tides! She turned round and clambered up onto the highest rock she could find - for what else could she do? Then she sat down and tried to work out how long she might have to wait before the tide went out again. It was clear now that the interval between high and low water here was less than six and a quarter hours – the figure which her calculation had been based upon. But anything much more than even five and a half would still mean waiting till it was nearly dark. She would certainly be missed back at the house long before that and cause no end of worry. As for the smugglers, they would surely have returned by then. So it seemed that she had little choice: she would have to throw herself on their mercy, if she was not to spend the whole night in the cave. She had been caught between the devil and the deep blue sea.

To distract herself while she waited, Hoglinda cast her mind back to the previous evening. Based on the conversation she had overheard, she reckoned that Quiller was probably the smuggler-in-chief. Certainly Mr Cutliss was the ship's captain, who had brought the contraband over the sea; and Mr Tubby was responsible for unloading it. Gradually everything was falling into place. Despite her situation she felt a curious satisfaction at being able to work it out. But then she suddenly remembered something Mr Cutliss had said to Mr Tubby, and a chill ran down her spines.

"Let's hope you're not caught out by the spring tide," he had said. It was the spring tide which had made it possible for her to visit the cave in the first place. But, of course, a spring tide also meant extreme high water – high enough for Mr Cutliss to worry that the cave would flood, damaging the contraband. Hoglinda was now worried for her own survival.

Getting to her feet, she looked around desperately, without knowing what she was looking for. She briefly considered retreating to the inner cave, but the thought of being trapped there filled her with horror. Perhaps she could find some driftwood to cling to. Shielding her eyes against the sun, she searched the incoming waves, hoping to spot a stick or two or even a plank, if she was lucky. Instead, she spotted something much better. There was a small boat coming across the bay, rowed by a single hedgehog. Of course, he might be a smuggler, too; but she could see no other way out.

"Ahoy there!" she shouted as loudly as she could, waving her hat to catch his attention.

He looked up. "Don't move!" he shouted back. "I shall be with you directly."

He turned the boat and began to row vigorously in her direction. A few minutes later she was safe on board and heading back to the shore.

"Thank you, sir - from the bottom of my heart. I believe I owe you my life, for I cannot swim."

"How came you to be there?" asked the stranger.

"I was er..." Hoglinda hesitated. She picked a piece of seaweed off her skirt and emptied the water from her boots, to give herself time to think. But what could she say? The stranger must have noticed the contraband at the back of the cave. Yet he had said nothing about it. Perhaps he *was* one of them. And if he was not? Well, she had no wish to confide in him, however much she disapproved of her cousin's smuggling. She would just have to pretend that she had stumbled upon the cave and its contents by accident. "Oh, I was just out walking," she said at last, "exploring the bay, and the cave entrance looked so magnificent I was curious to see inside. I was astonished when I found it was a smugglers' hiding place! But perhaps I should not be surprised - I am told that smuggling is commonplace on the Back."

"Yes, it is," said the stranger matter-of-factly. "And did you not see the tide coming in?"

"No, I..." Hoglinda hesitated again. "Well, to be honest, I was hiding from the smugglers, for they suddenly turned up and I was frightened.

Then, by the time they had gone, the tide had turned." She looked at him to see how he would react, but he was giving nothing away.

"I see," said the stranger. "Well, no doubt you will be more careful in future... But let me introduce myself. I am Snipwicke of Bristlestone Mill."

"And I am Hoglinda, daughter of Admiral Hoglander."

"Admiral Hoglander?" repeated Snipwicke, who knew of her father by name - the island was proud of its only admiral. "Then you are far from home."

"No, for my father is gone to the colonies to put down the rebellion there. I am now living with my cousin, who lives not more than a mile and a half from here."

"And how do you like it on the Back?"

"I like it very well. That is to say, it is certainly as beautiful as anything we have around Brambling, but I confess I would like it better if there were more hedgehogs of my own age and..." She was about to say 'class' but stopped herself. Being a hedgehog of her own time, she was conscious of social distinctions but not tactless. "Mr Snipwicke," she said, altering tack. "I think I must have caused you a great inconvenience. You were headed in the other direction, were you not?"

"It is no matter."

"That I cannot believe. I am sure you must have better ways of spending your time than rescuing damsels in distress. You were, after all, headed *somewhere*, were you not?"

"I assure you, Miss Hoglinda, that nothing could be more important to me than saving a hedgehog from drowning."

"But what brings you out to sea?" asked Hoglinda. "I presume you must be a miller, if you live at Bristlestone Mill - is that so?"

"Yes," said Snipwicke, smiling. "In fact, I've been delivering flour to some customers in Hog's Edge and I was just on my way back home, that is all."

Hoglinda eyed Snipwicke with fresh suspicion. She thought it unlikely the locals would want to buy their flour from Bristlestone Mill, when there was a perfectly good mill in Hog's Edge. She glanced at his jacket. There was not a speck of flour either on him or anywhere in the boat. She concluded that he was most probably lying. But, of course, she was herself unwilling to tell the whole truth. So she fell silent, and they did not speak again until they reached the shore. Then, helping her out of the boat, he offered to walk her home. She thanked him but refused as politely as she could. It was bad enough that her dress was damp and crumpled. She had no wish to turn up on Quiller's doorstep in the company of a stranger, for it might lead to questions she preferred not to answer.

When she reached the house, she found Pinafore working in the garden. There was no sign of the hoglets, however, though it was a beautiful day and very warm for April; this would usually be enough to bring them outside.

"How are Quillemina and Quillip?" she asked.

Pinafore glanced at Hoglinda's dress but was not so impertinent as to remark upon it. "They be gone for a walk with Mrs Brush, ma'am. It seems they han't caught no cold aater all."

"I am very glad to hear it," replied Hoglinda. She felt a little guilty for jumping to such a convenient conclusion but could not regret it.

"And Mr Quiller? Is he returned yet?"

"Oh, no, ma'am. I don't expect the master'll be back afore evening."

Hoglinda entered the house. Having escaped any awkward questions, she was now tempted to try her luck again. Discovering Quiller's secret had only made her want to know more, and being alone in the house was too good an opportunity to miss. As soon as she had changed into some dry clothes, she grabbed a candle and went down to the study. The loose section of wooden panelling had been put back. Indeed, she would never have guessed it *could* be removed, had she not seen this for herself. Yet, knowing what she did, she found she could lift it out again without too much difficulty.

The secret chamber, which had been virtually empty just a few hours ago, was now piled high with contraband. This was indisputable evidence of her cousin's guilt. She put the wooden panelling back in place and then turned her attention to Quiller's desk. The drawer was locked, but a quick search of the room revealed the key, hidden behind the clock on the mantelpiece. In the drawer she found letters, copies of letters, promissory notes, a purse and a notebook. She moved the contents onto the desk and then pawed through the items one by one.

The notebook was a ledger: a record of payments made, received or owing for all kinds of goods from wine and tea to cloth - all goods heavily taxed by the government. The smugglers, of course, paid no tax. Indeed, they liked to call themselves 'Free Traders', but in Hoglinda's opinion they were no better than thieves. While hedgehogs like her father, Admiral Hoglander, risked their lives for their country, the smugglers cheated the government out of the money needed to pay for the navy. It disgusted her to think that Quiller was one of them.

			£	S	D
Jan. 27th	Mrs Tipps				
Jan. 27th	port wine	40 ankers	160	0	0
Jan. 27th	claret	24 ankers	96	11	11
	geneva	32 ankers	128	11	11
Jan. 28th	Mr Rollup				
Jan. 28th	tobacco	4 lbs	3	0	0
	brandy	1/2 anker	1	4	11
n. 29th	Mrs Prickles				
29th	tea	2 lbs	0	1	4
29th	silk stockings	1 pair	3	2	11
	lace	1 yard	0	13	10
	Mr Thistle				
29th	claret	1/2 anker	4	2	6

Hoglinda turned her attention to the pile of letters; by reading through them, she gradually managed to piece together a rough picture of Quiller's smuggling activities. His active involvement seemed to date from his purchase of a ship, the *Hogspur*. He had bought this together with Mr Cutliss, who was also the ship's captain, just as she had suspected. The *Hogspur* had been built at the shipyard near Brambling Harbour the previous autumn, and this had been the reason for Quiller's visit to her father's house at the time. Until now, however, Hoglinda had always assumed the purchase was a simple financial investment. It had, of course, never occurred to her that he would use the *Hogspur* for smuggling.

His involvement with smugglers, however, seemed to go back much further than the purchase of his ship. Many of his letters were to or from merchants in Gruntsey. Gruntsey was another island, but far away across the sea, and it looked as though this was where not only Quiller but many other smugglers went to buy their contraband; for it was an important trading centre, selling everything from wine grown in nearby Furze to tea shipped in from far away lands in the East. It seemed that Quiller – being a fairly wealthy hedgehog – had for some years now acted as a banking agent between these Gruntsey merchants

and the smugglers. Any smugglers he knew and vouched for were allowed to collect their goods without paying for them straightaway. Then, after they had sold the goods on to their customers on the Isle of Needles, Quiller would collect the money from them and send it to the Gruntsey merchants on their behalf – in return for a small payment.

The last letter in the pile was of a quite different nature. It was from none other than Mr Snipwicke, the hedgehog who had rescued Hoglinda from the cave. In the letter, Snipwicke accused Quiller of deliberately selling his cargo for less than it was worth, so he could put him out of business and steal his customers. So Snipwicke *was* a smuggler, just as she had suspected. But the accusation he made astonished and shocked her. Indeed, she found it hard to believe, despite everything she had just learnt about her cousin. Having herself experienced only kindness from Quiller, she could not believe him that bad. Of course, she knew nothing of Mr Snipwicke. It was perfectly possible his accusation was false. And at least his letter reassured her on one front: he was unlikely to tell Quiller about her visit to the cave.

Hoglinda put the letters and other items back in Quiller's desk as she had found them and returned the key to its hiding place. Then she went up to her room to think. She had to decide what to do with all this information. She was angry with Quiller. There were no two ways about it: he was a criminal and he was cheating the government out of a lot of money. But he was also her cousin, he had welcomed her into his home and, what was more, he was the father of two young hoglets. She could not bring herself to betray him to the Customs Service - the authority responsible for both collecting taxes and catching smugglers. She wondered if she should leave. But to return to her father's empty house - to cast herself adrift from her cousin without explanation, she could imagine the gossip that would cause. In any case, she felt it was her duty to put a stop to Quiller's smuggling and force him to live honestly. She considered confronting him with what she had learnt and shaming him into changing his ways; but she doubted he would take much notice, being so much older and more experienced in the world than she was. And, if he refused to change his ways, what then? She could hardly remain in his house, as though nothing had happened. Gradually, a new idea formed in her mind - a terrifying idea, for she knew Quiller would never forgive her, if he discovered she was responsible. But her father had always taught her to do right and fear no hedgehog. So she made up her mind to do it: she would sink the *Hogspur*.

31

Chapter Three
26th April 1777: evening

It was around seven o'clock in the evening when Hoglinda set off back to Hog's Head Bay, this time taking with her a lantern and a bag of tools she had found in an out-building. By the time she arrived, the light was beginning to fade. A little while longer and there should be little risk of being observed. Sitting down on the beach to wait, she gazed out towards the *Hogspur*. She was a medium-sized lugger and would not be easy to sink. Hoglinda began to have doubts. Indeed, the deliberate wrecking of a ship was a terrible thing - indefensible unless to prevent a greater crime. She wondered whether she ought to give up her idea and go home. Yet somehow it seemed easier to stay where she was than to make up her mind to leave.

So she stayed. She watched the tide come in, pause and turn. She watched the sun slip below the horizon, leaving just a faint glow in its wake. As darkness descended, she began to feel as though her decision had already been made. She got up and walked over to some rowing boats which had been pulled up onto the beach. Looking around to check she was unobserved, she pushed one of the boats down to the sea. Then she climbed in, grabbed the oars and began to row. It was hard work, and the *Hogspur* seemed an awfully long way off. But eventually she came alongside - around the back, where her boat

would be out of sight from the shore. She boarded the *Hogspur* hesitantly, listening out for voices; but there was no one there. It was a strange eerie feeling, all alone on a deserted ship in the twilight - a ship where she had no business to be. Shivers of fear ran down her spines. But there was no going back now.

Hoglinda lit her lantern and quickly descended the ladder into the hold. Then, selecting a spot below the water line, she set to work with a pickaxe. As she struck at the wood again and again, the sound of the blows was uncomfortably loud. It was so loud that she never heard the crew coming on board.

"Drop the axe!" said a voice behind her.

Hoglinda dropped it at once, more in shock than obedience. Twisting round, she was confronted by a group of four hedgehogs. One of them had a pistol in his paw. It was pointed straight at her.

"What's the meaning of this?" he barked. "Who are you? Who sent you?"

Hoglinda hesitated. She recognized his voice from the conversation in Quiller's parlour: this was Mr Cutliss, the *Hogspur's* captain.

"Why, 'tes clear as day!" said the hedgehog to his left. "She be in the pay o' the Preventives!" 'Preventives' was another term for the Customs Service.

"No, that's not it - 'tedden't the way o' the Preventives, this," said another. "I reckons she be worken' for a rival gang."

"No!" she protested, trembling with fear. "I have nothing to do with the Preventives or any rival gang. It was my own choice to come here."

"Why?" asked the first hedgehog.

"Throw 'er over the side!" said another from the back of the group, and one of his companions echoed his wishes.

"No, please! I beg you!" pleaded Hoglinda. "I cannot swim!"

"You should have thought of that afore you come," said the hedgehog who had threatened her.

"Enough!" said Cutliss. "I wants to hear what she's got to say for herself. Well?"

"My name's Hoglinda. I'm Mr Quiller's cousin." There were gasps of surprise, but no one said anything. "When I found out about his smuggling, I... I... Well, it's wrong - it's against the law. So I felt I had to stop him. I knew he wouldn't listen to me, but I wasn't going to inform on him. So I decided to scuttle his ship instead."

Cutliss lowered his weapon. "So, you're Mr Quiller's cousin, are you? Well, we'll have to see what he has to say about this - though there's more than Mr Quiller what's got an interest in the *Hogspur*." He turned to the hedgehog who had just accused her of working for a rival gang. "Pinaft, take a look at the damage."

Pinaft looked. "Oh, it don't look too bad, skipper. In fact, I reckons we can fix 'n in a trice."

"Well, that's lucky for you then, Miss Hoglinda," said the captain. "Some of us has got a terrible quick temper." He turned to Pinaft. "Take Miss Hoglinda to see Mr Quiller. It'll give you a chance to catch up with that sister of yourn."

Pinaft protested. "But I thought you wanted - "

"No, no, we'll manage without you," interrupted Cutliss, who was understandably reluctant to discuss their business in front of Hoglinda.

Pinaft made no further protest, but escorted Hoglinda back to her boat and rowed her ashore. They set off in silence, but in the end Hoglinda felt she must say something.

"I believe Mr Cutliss said you had a sister, Pinaft. Is that right?"

"What d'you want to know for?" asked Pinaft suspiciously.

"I was just trying to be friendly."

"What for? You cares nothing for the likes of we. You... you be so high and mighty - making yourself judge and jury over us all."

"That isn't fair!" protested Hoglinda. "Smuggling is against the law - you know it is!"

"The law!" scoffed Pinaft. "That's for rich folks like yourself. You wouldn't think the same if you had to live paw-to-mouth on a shillen' a day." He watched the look of surprise on her face. A shilling a day was less than £16 a year. Her own allowance was £120 a year and that was just for clothes and amusements. "That's right," he continued. "That's what you makes from fishen' - if you be lucky. And, as soon as you tries to bring in a more valuable cargo, then the government bleeds you dry."

Hoglinda was silent. It had never occurred to her that many of the smugglers acted out of necessity. When she had found out that Quiller was a smuggler, she had of course been right to be angry with him - for *he* surely acted out of greed. Though not rich like Admiral Hoglander, he still lived comfortably enough. He received a good enough income from his land not to have to work at all and certainly had no need to smuggle. But the circumstances of hedgehogs like Pinaft and his companions were clearly very different. Though it was difficult to forget their boarish behaviour towards her and the violence which some of them had threatened her with, she at least began to understand them a little better.

"I am sorry," she said at last. "I did not realize... When I tried to scuttle the *Hogspur,* I was thinking only of my cousin, which was wrong of me. Truly, I am sorry."

"So you'll not go tryen' summat like that again?"

She shook her head. At this, her companion softened, and the walk back to Hog's Edge passed without any further hostility. Hoglinda even managed to discover that Pinaft's sister was none other than Quiller's housemaid, Pinafore.

When they reached Quiller's house, Hoglinda hoped she would be allowed to make her confession to Quiller in private. However, Pinaft insisted on accompanying her into the parlour. Quiller was at his desk, writing. He looked up as they stepped into the room and, seeing them together, frowned.

"What's this?" he asked. "What's going on?"

"Sorry to trouble you, Mr Quiller, sir, but we thought as you'd want to know. We found Miss Hoglinda on board the *Hogspur.*"

"On board the *Hogspur*? Why? What on earth were you doing there?" Quiller's questions were directed at his cousin.

Hoglinda felt all the awkwardness of the situation, yet there was a note of defiance in her voice as she replied. "I was going to scuttle her," she said, boldly.

"What!" exclaimed Quiller, rising from his seat.

"Don't you worry, sir. We stopped en afore she done much damage. 'Tes easily mended."

"I am very pleased to hear it," said Quiller, sinking back into his seat. "Well, Pinaft," he added pointedly, "I imagine you must be impatient to see your sister."

Pinaft took the hint and left the cousins on their own, closing the door behind him.

Quiller looked at Hoglinda tetchily. "Well, aren't you going to sit down?"

Hoglinda sat but did not speak.

"Now perhaps you can tell me, cousin, why exactly you were going to scuttle my ship."

"Because you are using her to break the law. Because smuggling is wrong."

"I see," said Quiller, bristling with irritation. "And why - if you were so very upset about my activities - did you not speak to me about it?"

"Because I knew that nothing I could say would make you change your mind."

"You *knew*, did you?" responded Quiller, who seemed angrier than ever. Then he reflected for a moment. "Well, I dare say you were right - for why should I? And, after everything I have done for you - after welcoming you into my home, Hoglinda, I would have expected more gratitude."

"I *am* grateful," protested Hoglinda. "Really I am. But that does not change the fact that you are breaking the law. Quiller, surely you must see that smuggling is wrong. You are cheating the government out of its taxes - the money the navy needs for the war in the colonies - and the army."

"So you are thinking of my Uncle Hoglander, are you? That does you credit, but I'm afraid the war in the colonies can never be won. Really, it's a hopeless case. The government is throwing away its money on a lost cause."

"My father does not think so. He writes saying the Bristlish and the Loyalists have the upper paw."

"For now it may appear so," responded Quiller, "but our good fortune cannot last. We stand alone; the rebels do not. Everyone knows the Furzish Navy sends weapons to the rebels. And it is only a matter of time before the Furzish government declares war on us. Then we shall be fighting on two fronts - against the rebels in the colonies, and against the Furzish right here on our doorstep."

"I think my father is better placed than *you* to make that judgement," insisted Hoglinda. "In any case, it is still the government's money."

Quiller shook his head. "I disagree. Who pays for the cargo? We do. Who risks their lives running the cargo across the sea? We do. We work hard for our money. And many among us would struggle to survive if we could not trade freely."

"But not you!" said Hoglinda. "You could live very comfortably without smuggling."

"So what would you have me do? Set myself above my friends? While they risk their lives and their freedom, am I to live a quiet and comfortable life, untroubled by the poverty all around me? Am I not to lift a paw to help them? No, that won't do! No hedgehog is an island, and I will not abandon my friends."

Hoglinda was silent. Quiller seemed to have an answer for everything; he made her sound unreasonable and unfeeling. She felt he must surely despise her. But then he appeared to read her thoughts, for he softened a little.

"I am sorry, Hoglinda. I spoke harshly. I know it is difficult for you to understand: you have lived a sheltered life. My Uncle Hoglander clearly wishes to protect you from any unpleasantness. Why, I suppose he never told you from whom he bought his own excellent collection of wines."

Hoglinda looked at Quiller, aghast at his insinuation. Her father was an admiral. What was more, he had dined several times with Mr Gimlet, the Preventive officer. "Are you accusing my father of buying smuggled wine?" she asked.

"It is not an accusation," said Quiller. "Indeed, I can assure you it is quite true, for I sold him the wine myself."

Hoglinda felt crushed. Her father had let her down. She was angry with him and ashamed of having been so blind and foolish. "Well," she said, clutching at straws, "I don't suppose it ever occurred to him that his own nephew was a smuggler."

"Oh, he knows all right," said Quiller, "for I have never made any pretence about it. But you must understand, Hoglinda, that your father has done nothing wrong - nothing at all. Why, there is scarcely a hedgehog on the island who is not involved in the Trade, one way or another."

Chapter Four
April 1777 to January 1778

Over the following days, Hoglinda came to accept that she had been wrong to condemn the smugglers. Gradually, she became used to Quiller's way of life. She even got to know some of the smugglers who visited the house. This was not just the crew of the *Hogspur* and Mr Tubby's shore party but others, too, from Hog's Edge village and beyond. Many independent smugglers relied upon Quiller's services. Sometimes, however, they just came seeking his help as a neighbour. Quiller was clearly held in high regard throughout the neighbourhood and, whenever times were bad, he could be counted on to lend others a helping paw.

Gently - almost without noticing it - Hoglinda was drawn into Quiller's murky world. At first she was motivated purely by charity. If she learned that a smuggler or one of his family had fallen sick or was otherwise in distress, she would visit them. Occasionally Quiller would then ask her to pass on a message for him while she was there or if she happened to be passing a smuggler's cottage on one of her walks. But, once she had earned his trust, he came to rely upon her more and more. And it was not long before she was collecting payments for him and even delivering small packets of contraband, such as lace or gloves. Gradually, she learned the ropes of the Trade. And when she learnt that Pinafore was carrying smuggled wine beneath her skirts, she volunteered to do the same.

Much to her surprise, these were happy days for Hoglinda. The pleasure of being useful, after a lifetime of comfortable idleness, was greater than she could possibly have imagined. And, though a strange sense of unease still lingered at the back of her mind, she put this down to her upbringing and paid as little attention to it as possible. Quiller, for his part, was happy to involve his cousin in his affairs. She was a good worker; and, now that she had joined him on the wrong side of the law, he no longer feared that she might betray him.

The months passed. As spring turned to summer, business tailed off a little. It was always during the summer that the smugglers had it hardest. Long days and fair weather made the Preventives' job a great deal easier. But, with the arrival of autumn, the smugglers once again had the upper paw. Soon they were as busy as ever. Hoglinda continued to carry messages for them, collect payments and deliver contraband. As time went on, Quiller's business took her further and

further afield. Sometimes it seemed to her as though his smuggling business would eventually expand to cover the whole of the Isle of Needles.

As though to confirm this thought, one day in October, Quiller asked her to make a delivery to a new customer in Bristlestone, a village lying some considerable distance from Hog's Edge. The customer in question was the rector at the local church, the Reverend Mr Humble, who probably should have been above such things. But she was not surprised. She was beginning to learn that Quiller had been right, when he had said there was scarcely a hedgehog on the island who was not involved in the Trade.

Hoglinda set off at daybreak. By the time the sun appeared above the horizon, she was already up on the downs. Despite the weight of the wine she was carrying, she walked briskly and took pleasure in her outing. It was a beautiful day; and almost the whole of the south-west coast was stretched out before her - a patchwork of fields, hedges and woods, and beyond it the silver sea.

On reaching Bristlestone, she turned down the little wooded lane leading to the rectory and was pausing to remove a stone from her boot, when someone called out to her.

"Miss Hoglinda!"

40

She looked up. It was Mr Snipwicke, who had rescued her from the cave six months earlier. Though they had not met since, she had not forgotten the hedgehog to whom she owed her life.

"Mr Snipwicke!" she said, going down the lane to meet him. "What a lovely surprise to see you here! But perhaps I should not be surprised, for this is your village, is it not?"

"Yes, Bristlestone Mill is just below this field," he said, pointing down the lane. "But *you* are a long way from home." He hesitated. "May I ask what brings you here?"

"I have business at the rectory."

"The rectory?" repeated Snipwicke, who seemed both surprised and a little put out. "Why, I am, myself, just come from the rectory. Might I ask the nature of your business there?"

Again he spoke hesitantly. No doubt he was remembering the awkwardness of their first meeting, when neither of them had told the other the full truth. But, of course, a lot had changed since then. What had once appeared to Hoglinda to be a shameful secret now seemed quite ordinary to her. Smuggling had become a part of her everyday life. And, of course, she now knew that Snipwicke was a smuggler, too. So, whatever the ill-feeling between him and her cousin, they were hardly likely to inform on each other, for they were both equally guilty in the sight of the law.

"I am come on behalf of my cousin," said Hoglinda, "to deliver some wine to the rector."

"I see," said Snipwicke, a little crossly for, since their last meeting, he had found out exactly who her cousin was. "Well, that explains my own lack of success today. I couldn't understand why the rector did not wish to renew his regular order. Clearly your cousin has undercut me - again."

Hoglinda suddenly remembered the letter she had found from Mr Snipwicke to Quiller. In it, Snipwicke had made a similar accusation but had gone much further. He had accused Quiller of cutting his prices *deliberately* and to even less than the contraband was worth in order to steal his customers. Hoglinda bristled. She was no more willing to believe this of her cousin now than she had been then.

"If your prices are too high, Mr Snipwicke, you have only to lower them," she said defensively.

"I can assure you my prices are low already. Indeed, I can go no lower. Frankly, it beats me how your cousin can afford to do it."

There was an awkward silence between the two hedgehogs. Then Hoglinda excused herself and went on her way. But, on her journey back home, she found her thoughts returning to Mr Snipwicke and his repeated accusations against her cousin. So far she had only ever had *his* side of the story.

"I met Mr Snipwicke this morning," she said to Quiller, as they sat down to dinner that afternoon.

"Mr Snipwicke? I didn't know the two of you were acquainted."

Fortunately, Quiller was not interested enough to ask how they had met, so Hoglinda offered no explanation.

"He said the rector at Bristlestone used to buy his wine from him," she said.

"What of it?" asked Quiller, barely looking up from his meal.

"He says you undercut him."

"Snipwicke's trouble," said Quiller tetchily, putting down his knife and fork, "is that he's too ambitious. He simply has no idea of his own limitations. He is a first-rate sailor - as good as any I know, I grant you, but he has a poor head for business. He should stick to what he knows and leave the rest to others."

"You mean to you?"

"Well, yes. And why not? I have the capital and the connections. In fact, if he is struggling for money, I would be happy to buy the *Sea Urchin* from him. She's a fine little boat and would complement the *Hogspur* nicely. I'd be prepared to make him a good offer, which should easily clear his debts."

"Oh, I didn't know he was in debt," said Hoglinda. She reflected for a moment. "If you bought the *Sea Urchin,* would you keep him on as her captain?"

"Of course. Why would I not?"

That seemed to be an end of the matter. Hoglinda soon forgot about Snipwicke and concentrated instead on matters which concerned her more closely. This included her own role in Quiller's smuggling, which seemed to grow with every passing month. It began to occur to Hoglinda that she had nothing to show for all her work. She felt it would be pleasing to receive *something* in recognition of all the risks she ran. It was not that she wished to be paid. That would be unreasonable, when Quiller received her in his home for nothing. In any case, paid employment would hardly be appropriate for the daughter of an admiral. But a financial investment would, she felt, be perfectly respectable; and, if all went well, she would then take a share of the profits along with Quiller and the other investors.

So when in December Quiller started to plan his next smuggling run, Hoglinda offered to contribute some of her own money to the costs. Quiller accepted her offer. With a large-scale business such as his, it was always better to share the risk - rather than a single hedgehog face ruin if his ship were wrecked or captured.

And so it was that, on the first day of the new year, Hoglinda found herself sitting down with Quiller and his smuggling partners in order to discuss their next venture. Besides Quiller himself, there was Mr Cutliss, captain and joint owner of the *Hogspur* - the very hedgehog who had caught Hoglinda trying to sink the *Hogspur*, that fateful night so many months ago. There was Mrs Tipps, the innkeeper at the Hog's Head Inn. She was responsible for diluting and colouring the brandy before it was sold on - this was necessary to make it drinkable. She was also, of course, an important customer herself. Then there was a rather portly hedgehog called Mr Tubby, who was in charge of the shore party. Hoglinda was the youngest by far. She felt both nervous and excited.

Quiller opened the meeting. "I have here a letter," he announced, "from Monsieur Pinot in Gruntsey. He is offering wine at one pound

an anker, brandy at the same price and tea at seven pence a pound, *if* we'll collect before the end of January. I therefore - "

"But surely, Mr Quiller," interrupted Tubby, "it don't make no sense to do another run so soon? We've still goods left over from our last run to sell. We'd do much better to wait till February."

Quiller shook his head. "If we delay, we shan't get as good a price again. Time and tide wait for no hedgehog, Mr Tubby. Besides, I have found some new customers and, if the price is low, we shall sell it quickly enough." He looked around at the others, as though silently commanding them to agree. Cutliss and Mrs Tipps both nodded.

"So I be outvoted then," said Tubby grumpily, for he knew that Quiller always got his own way sooner or later. "Well, I suppose, if we *must* do it, then I better come up with somewhere to put it all, seeing as all our usual places be full - Mottlestone churchyard, the manor and, of course, your own hiding place here, Mr Quiller... Oh, I suppose Furry Barn in Bristlestone village might do or the churchyard in Sharpwell. But that's an awful long way to carry it all - unless, of course, Mr Cutliss, you be willen' to bring the *Hogspur* into Bristlestone Bay."

"But is that not Mr Snipwicke's beach?" asked Hoglinda.

"He uses it; it is not *his* beach," said Quiller pointedly. "However, as it happens, Bristlestone Bay would not serve our purpose on this occasion, for I am planning to sell half the cargo on the mainland. From Hog's Head Bay, you see, we can use the River Hogwash to transport it to the north coast, ready for onward shipment to the mainland. That'll be organized by a Mr Pawter of Sowfleet."

"And who be Mr Pawter?" asked Tubby.

"A new acquaintance of mine. He has recently moved over from Pawsmouth and retains some useful connections on the mainland."

"Overners," growled Tubby. 'Overners' was the local term for mainlanders who came to settle on the Isle of Needles. Tubby was suspicious of anyone from the mainland.

"That's right, Mr Tubby," responded Quiller. "An overner who is willing to pay a good price, so we shall do well out of him."

"Perhaps," said Tubby, "but we still have the rest of the cargo to take away. If my hedgehogs have to carry it all the way from Hog's Head Bay to Bristlestone, 'tes goen' to cost more, an' who's goen' to pay for that? *I* can't. Why, I'll be hard put to pay more than a shillen' into this run, so soon aater the last one."

"I can pay for it, Mr Tubby," said Hoglinda. Suddenly all eyes were upon her. Tubby, Cutliss and Mrs Tipps had all been wondering why Quiller had invited her to their meeting, but no one had liked to ask. Now that they knew, Hoglinda could not tell whether they were pleased or not. "Of course," she said, a little discouraged by their silence, "if you would prefer... I mean, if someone else wants to take this on instead of me, then I - "

"No, no, Hoglinda," said Quiller, before any of the others could respond. "You have as much right to invest in this run as any of us. You have earned your place at this table."

"And you be very welcome in our little group, Miss Hoglinda," said Mrs Tipps warmly.

"Most welcome indeed," echoed Tubby with a smile - his grumpiness apparently forgotten.

Only Cutliss looked at Hoglinda suspiciously but then he seemed to remember himself. "Why, yes, of course," he said hastily, with a curt nod. Hoglinda felt that he had never really trusted her, ever since their first unfortunate meeting on board the *Hogspur*.

"Good," said Quiller. "So that is settled then. Now I should perhaps mention, Mr Cutliss, that I shall be sailing with you on this occasion. I have some unfinished business to attend to in Gruntsey, but I shall not detain you long. A day is all I need at most."

"It'll be a pleasure to have you on board, Mr Quiller. When do you wish to go? We've a good run of dark nights ahead – as far as the 15th, in fact. But, if you're in a hurry, we can get ready to sail within the next couple o' days. The choice is yourn."

"Well, I shall need to be in St Pricklier Port either on January the 8th or soon after."

"If that be the case," said Cutliss, "then let's sail on the 7th. With a fair wind, we should arrive in St Pricklier Port the following day. Then, if we aims to depart on the 9th, we'll have plenty of leeway - if we're delayed for some reason or other." Here Cutliss paused to consult his journal. "The following night, the night of the 10th, high water's at twenty minutes past eleven o'clock. So, Mr Tubby, if you could have your look-outs ready to return our signal at a quarter afore ten, that'd do very nicely."

"Certainly, Mr Cutliss," responded Tubby. "I'll post three hedgehogs on the cliff tops as usual – one above the cave at Hog's Head Bay, one over at Crumbley and a third at Whiskercombe. And, of course, Mrs Tipps here will light a candle in an upper window of the inn, so as to signal the coast be clear, just as she always does."

Mrs Tipps nodded her agreement but made no comment.

"But what if you should arrive early, Mr Cutliss?" asked Hoglinda, who was trying to understand how everything came together.

"Then we'll stand off - that is to say, Miss Hoglinda, we shall keep away from the shore - till the appointed hour. We shall not, in any case, make land afore nightfall."

"And we can rely upon the *Hogspur's* usual crew?" asked Quiller.

"Oh, yes, sir, they're only waiting for the word."

"And what about you, Mr Tubby?" asked Quiller. "I assume that, with the right money, there should be no difficulty recruiting enough tub carriers for the night. What do you suggest we offer them?"

Tubby reflected for a moment. "Oh, I'd say about ten shillings apiece for the night. That should do the trick."

"But how many hedgehogs will you employ, Mr Tubby?" asked Hoglinda. Remembering Pinaft's complaint that a day's fishing had earned him a shilling at most, she thought ten shillings each seemed rather a lot.

"Oh, I don't reckon as we'll need above sixty hedgehogs," said Tubby. "That'd come to thirty pounds in all. Tain't too much for you, Miss Hoglinda, is it?"

"No, I..." Hoglinda hesitated, glancing at Quiller to see whether he approved.

Quiller shook his head again. "Your generosity does you credit, Mr Tubby, but there is no need to overdo it. Sixty hedgehogs indeed! Many paws make light work, but no one pays a hedgehog ten shillings for light work. What is more, we would wipe out the benefit of the low prices we've been offered by Monsieur Pinot. No, let us say... eight shillings apiece and forty hedgehogs. Shall we?"

"Well, t'won't be easy to recruit 'em," said Tubby. Then he shrugged. "But I expects I'll manage if I have to."

"Thank you, Mr Tubby. Now, added to our other costs, that brings our total overheads to two hundred and seventy-two pounds, three shillings and tuppence. Well, my friends, I think that finishes our business for the day."

"But what of me?" asked Hoglinda. "I have nothing to do. Surely I could be of some use to someone?"

"My dear," said Mrs Tipps. " 'Teddn't for the likes of we to go creepen' round in the middle o' the night."

"She's quite right, cousin," said Quiller. "This is no game we are playing. My uncle would not thank me if I let you take such risks."

"But I already take risks - a great many. No doubt my father would disapprove of that too. I really cannot see the difference."

"Yet the difference is great indeed," said Quiller. "The difference, in fact, between day and night, for the Preventives are likely to question any hedgehog they catch prowling around the coast after dark... No, I am sorry, Hoglinda, the risk would be too great. I cannot allow it. If you were arrested, what would I say to your father?"

Hoglinda saw it was useless to protest, but her frustration was enormous. She was surprised that she felt so strongly about it. Not so long ago, she had done her best to put a stop to Quiller's smuggling. But now that she was involved herself, she found that she enjoyed it more than anything else. She loved the activity and the excitement and, above all, the sense of purpose it gave her.

When the time came for the *Hogspur* to set sail, leaving Hoglinda at home with no role to play, she found it hard to put her mind to anything. Many an hour was wasted sitting upon the shore gazing out to sea. She tried to imagine the voyage, the bustling quayside at St

Pricklier Port, where the cargo would be loaded, and the island of Gruntsey itself. From the little she knew of it, she thought Gruntsey must be very unlike her own island. The Gruntsey islanders were loyal to the same king, but that seemed to be where the similarity ended. While the Isle of Needles was part of Great Bristlin and lay just a little way off from the Bristlish mainland, Gruntsey was one of a cluster of islands far away across the sea. Indeed, it was closer to Furze than to Great Bristlin and, among themselves, the islanders spoke Furzish. Furthermore, being responsible for their own internal government, the Gruntsey islanders could trade openly with whomever they liked: *they* broke no law, unlike the smugglers themselves. Hoglinda thought it sounded such a fascinating and exciting place. If only she could have gone with her cousin...

Chapter Five
10th - 11th January 1778

January the 10th came round, and Hoglinda could scarcely sit still. When she heard a noise at the window, she jumped to her feet and pulled back the curtains - only to find that it was just a branch scraping against the glass. How foolish, she thought! It was only eight o'clock. The smugglers were not due back for another two hours. She sat down, but then got up again a moment later. Waiting up here at the house was impossible. She decided to go down to the bay and wait at the Hog's Head Inn, though she knew perfectly well that Quiller would not approve.

Hoglinda had sometimes wondered what the Hog's Head was like inside; but the public rooms of inns were rough places and generally considered to be no place for the female of the species. Mrs Tipps was different, of course, because she was the innkeeper; but for the daughter of an admiral to be seen in such a place was unthinkable. Hoglinda looked through her wardrobe, wondering whether her dark grey cloak, with the hood up, would be enough to conceal her identity. Then she remembered the old clothes she had discovered in Quiller's secret chest. Those would do very nicely. She crept into the study and, closing the door gently behind her, once again removed the panelling from beside the fireplace. Then, having swapped her elegant dress for a grubby pair of breeches, a thread-bare jacket and an old hat, she lit her lantern and stepped out into the night.

It was a cold night. A bitter wind penetrated through Hoglinda's tattered old clothing; she would undoubtedly have been a great deal warmer in her woollen cloak. A shiver ran down her spines. Was it the cold, she wondered, or nerves? With no moon to guide her, it was hardly the night to be venturing out alone for the very first time. Walking through the trees, she could see nothing beyond the small pool of light cast by her lantern. Who knew what might be lurking in the darkness? There were sounds everywhere - branches creaking in the wind, the screech of an owl... Twice she thought she heard a twig snap; but there was no one there - so far as she could tell.

As she neared the coast, the noise of the sea gradually overtook every other sound. Emerging from the woods behind Hog's Head Bay, she was pleased to find there was a stiff onshore breeze. The sea was a little rough, to be sure, but the smugglers would not mind that. Indeed, a little rough weather would give them the advantage, if they were unlucky enough to meet a Customs ship: for the smugglers were generally the better sailors; and, knowing the local coastline like the backs of their paws, they could take their boats where the Customs Service dared not follow.

Hoglinda searched the horizon, but there was nothing to see. If there were any boats out there, they were not showing a light; and even the sea itself seemed to merge into the moonless sky above. Towards the west end of the bay, however, she could just make out the faint silhouette of the Hog's Head Inn, punctured by the light from its two downstairs windows. She paused for a moment or two, listening to the waves breaking and retreating across the pebbles. Then she picked up her courage, pulled her hat down over her eyes and walked over to the inn.

The public room was a large, simply furnished place, bristling with hedgehogs. But, with a good fire going in the hearth, it was surprisingly cosy; and the drink was flowing freely - indeed, it was clear that more than one hedgehog was three sheets to the wind. Some of the customers she recognized from the village - including Mr Tubby, who was standing warming his paws by the fire. Fortunately, neither he nor anyone else saw through her disguise or even gave her a

50

second glance. So, finding herself an unoccupied table away from the light of the fire, she settled down to wait.

"What can I get 'ee, sir?" asked Mrs Tipps, coming over to her.

"A brandy, please," said Hoglinda, in a half whisper.

"What was that 'ee said? ...Crimany!" exclaimed Mrs Tipps, suddenly recognizing her. Slipping into the chair opposite, Mrs Tipps leant forward and lowered her voice. "Why, Miss Hoglinda, what *was* you thinken', comen' y'ere? Has summat happened?"

"No, Mrs Tipps - I just couldn't bear waiting on my own up at the house any longer. I know I should not have come."

Mrs Tipps shook her head disapprovingly. "No, ma'am, that you should not - "

"Hey there!" interrupted a disreputable-looking hedgehog from another table. Hoglinda noticed he was swaying a little, as though the chair beneath him were a tightrope. "What bist gossipen' about, Tippsy, wold dear? Casn't thee zee we be dyen' o' thirst over y'ere?"

"Drownen' in thee cups more like!" retorted Mrs Tipps, all the while leaping to her feet - for she was never one to say no to a customer. Scuttling off into a back room, she returned a minute later with the drinks. But neither she nor Hoglinda made any attempt to resume their conversation, for fear of attracting attention.

51

Time passed slowly once more for Hoglinda, sitting there on her own, surrounded by strangers and unable to talk to anyone. She dared not even check the watch in her pocket: only the wealthier sort of hedgehog could afford a timepiece and she was dressed as a pauper. She began to wish she had stayed at the house after all. If she carried through her plan and ventured out onto the beach when the *Hogspur* came in, she risked being challenged. Then she would have to reveal who she was, and Quiller would be angry again. He would probably send her home with her tail between her legs.

Here, however, Hoglinda's thoughts were interrupted, for the door was suddenly flung open. Silence descended upon the room. Two hedgehogs stood upon the threshold, one with a blood-stained cloth tied around his leg, who looked as though he was about to keel over. The other hedgehog Hoglinda recognized immediately: for, to her astonishment and horror, it was none other than Mr Gimlet, the Customs officer. She had met him several times when he had come to dine with her father. She tipped her hat a little further forward, hoping desperately that he would not recognize her.

"Some help here, if you please!" barked Gimlet, surveying Mrs Tipps's customers with barely concealed disgust. He was clearly having difficulty supporting his companion, but no one rose to help

52

him. Indeed, hostility was written on all their faces. As for Hoglinda, she was truly shocked. She wanted very much to help - especially as the wound must surely have been inflicted by one of Quiller's gang. Yet she dared not move a muscle. When Mr Gimlet looked in her direction, she wished she could just curl up into a ball.

"Help me, dammit!" bellowed Gimlet to the room. Mrs Tipps now came forward and shooed away one of her younger customers, who reluctantly gave up his chair. "No, that won't do!" said Gimlet crossly. "Can't you see that he has lost a great deal of blood? He must lie down. We'll take him upstairs."

"Oh, no, sir!" protested Mrs Tipps. Hoglinda thought she sounded a little too alarmed for her own good. "I'm sorry, sir," continued Mrs Tipps, "but all the rooms be taken. We best lay en down on the rug in the parlour, next door. 'Tes comfortable enough in there."

Ignoring her suggestion, Gimlet made a move towards the staircase, supporting his companion as best he could. When his companion gasped with pain, however, Hoglinda stood up instinctively. She regretted it at once, but it was too late for her to change her mind. So, taking the wounded hedgehog's other arm, she helped Gimlet escort him upstairs.

There were four doors leading off the landing. Hoglinda tried to steer them towards one of the rooms at the back, facing away from the

sea. But Gimlet had already opened the door to a bedroom at the front. On the windowsill was an unlit candle. A few minutes more and it would have been alight, signalling to the *Hogspur* that the coast was clear.

Hoglinda immediately looked away, fearing that Gimlet might follow her gaze. Then, as they laid the wounded hedgehog carefully upon the bed, Mrs Tipps appeared in the doorway, anxious and out of breath.

"Not y'ere," she said. "There be a room at the back you can have, ef you likes. But this room be taken."

Hoglinda edged towards the window and stood between it and Mr Gimlet, so the candle was hidden from his view.

"I thought you said they were *all* taken," said Gimlet sharply.

" 'Es, sir," said Mrs Tipps, apparently unabashed. " 'Tes jest that some be more taken than others."

Mrs Tipps had only succeeded in rousing his suspicions. Without asking her permission, he started to search the room, fully expecting to find some contraband hidden there or other evidence of smuggling. First he looked inside the cupboard. Then he knelt down to check under the bed. Quick as a flash, Mrs Tipps reached behind Hoglinda and popped the candlestick in her pocket.

"This room is empty," said Gimlet, rising to his feet. "Why did you say it was taken?" His gaze now wandered over to the windowsill, but he was too late.

"I be expecten' visitors," responded Mrs Tipps. "A gentlehog and his wife from over Boarchurch way. They be comen' tonight, an' this y'ere be their favourite room."

"What? Coming at this late hour?" queried Gimlet, but he did not wait for an answer. Though his suspicions remained, he had other more pressing matters to worry about. "Is there a physician in the village?" he asked.

"Not hereabouts," said Mrs Tipps. "The nearest be Dr Lancet at Hogmouth."

"Then send for him. In the meantime, you," said Gimlet, pointing a claw at Hoglinda, "stay with my colleague and look after him until the physician arrives." He turned to go but then paused. "His name is Snoach. What is yours?"

Hoglinda gawped at him, as she tried to think of a name. "Hoggin, sir," she said at last, adopting a broad accent and lowering her voice to make it sound as masculine as possible.

Gimlet frowned. "Hoggin, you say? Are you sure that's your real name? Your voice sounds strangely familiar... Yet I don't know anyone by that name... Take off your hat!"

Hoglinda had no choice, so she did as she was told. Gimlet scrutinized her face for several long seconds until she felt quite faint.

"Why, it is just as I thought!" he said triumphantly. "I *have* seen you somewhere before. And, as I doubt it was in a social capacity," he sneered, looking at her dirty old clothes, "I suppose I must have caught you smuggling somewhen. No matter, it will come back to me..."

Just then Snoach groaned, reminding Mr Gimlet that the hedgehogs who had shot him were still at large. "Well, Hoggin," he said, "when I return, I expect to find Mr Snoach no worse, or you will answer for it with your life. And, if Hoggin isn't your real name, be assured I will find you anyway - come hell or high water."

With that Gimlet hurried downstairs and was gone. Hoglinda gazed after him, half tempted to cut and run; but she could hardly leave Snoach unattended - it just would not be right. A second later, Mrs Tipps put her head round the door. Beckoning Hoglinda into the room opposite, she shut the door behind her.

"Oh, Mrs Tipps, what are we to do!" exclaimed Hoglinda, who was shocked by this turn of events. "I fear it was... Well, it must have been one of Mr Tubby's hedgehogs - one of ours - who shot poor Mr Snoach next door..."

"Indeed it must, my dear, but tain't no time for be'en squeamish. You should save your sympathy for the free-traders, who only wants to be left in peace. And, ef they do guard your money with their lives, be grateful."

"I *am* grateful," protested Hoglinda; but in truth she was no longer sure. Her mind was in a turmoil. She did not want *anyone* to get hurt - either the smugglers or the Preventives. "Do you think there is a risk some of our party will be caught?" she asked. "Is there someone we should warn?"

"No, don't you worry about that. Mr Tubby was y'ere when the Preventives arrived an' left as soon as they come upstairs. By now he'll have got the message out to anyone as what don't already know. So the best thing you can do, Miss Hoglinda, es stay with Mr Snoach next door and make sure he doesn't see nothen' what he eddn't supposed to see - while I attends to my customers."

With that, Mrs Tipps turned to go, but Hoglinda stopped her.

"Mrs Tipps," she asked anxiously, "you won't tell my cousin I was here, will you?"

"No, Miss Hoglinda, not ef he don't ask." And with that she was gone, returning only briefly, with a bowl of hot water and a couple of strips of cloth.

Hoglinda attended to her patient. Taking care to close the shutters and curtains first, she lit a candle. Then she put a fresh dressing on Snoach's leg, mopped his brow and occasionally, when he moaned in pain, held his paw. When eventually he fell into a deep sleep, she blew out the candle and, opening the curtains and shutters again, gazed out into the darkness. At a quarter to ten, there was a flash of light far out to sea - just a tiny pinprick of light, lasting less than a second. But to anyone looking that way it was unmistakable: the *Hogspur* was signalling her arrival. What would happen next, she wondered? With no candle alight in the window, Mr Cutliss certainly would not bring his boat into Hog's Head Bay. But would the neighbouring bays be any safer? Other Customs officers might be out there, besides Gimlet. The Customs Service might even have a ship lying in wait, ready to trap the returning smugglers.

Whatever the answers to these questions, Hoglinda guessed she would see little action tonight, for all her trouble. Perhaps it was just as well. She was now beginning to appreciate a little more the dangerous nature of smuggling. As Quiller had said, this was no game. Both sides risked their lives - not only the smugglers but the Preventives too. Yet the smugglers would never give up their Trade - it was simply too profitable. Neither would they risk capture, for the penalties if caught were severe. So they armed themselves, because the Preventives were armed. And, if they were cornered, bloodshed was almost inevitable. No doubt that was exactly what had happened tonight. Just thinking about it sent a shiver down Hoglinda's spines. Her earlier doubts about the morality of smuggling began to return. How could she have allowed herself to get so deeply involved? But this was no time to be thinking such thoughts. For tonight at least, she *was* involved and she would have to stay where she was. So, closing the shutters and curtains once more, she relit the candle and returned to Snoach's bedside.

At about half past ten Dr Lancet, the physician, finally arrived. It was with considerable relief that Hoglinda handed over the care of Mr Snoach. She now longed to be home. She got up to go, but then suddenly stopped, for she had just heard Quiller's voice on the landing. She paused in front of the door, her paw poised over the handle - prompting Dr Lancet to ask her whether something was wrong. She shook her head. Then, stepping away from the door, she enquired - almost in a whisper - whether the patient was likely to make a full recovery. Dr Lancet said something in response, but she scarcely heard him. Her attention was focussed instead on Quiller's voice; and, as soon as she heard the click of a door and was sure the coast was clear, she bade Dr Lancet an abrupt goodnight and left.

Out on the landing, Hoglinda could hear Quiller's voice coming from the room opposite. Though her first thought had been to get away as quickly as possible, her curiosity now got the better of her once more. She put her ear to the door. Yes, it was definitely Quiller speaking; but she could not make out what he was saying - until eventually it dawned upon her that he was speaking in Furzish. He spoke haltingly, with a poor accent. The hedgehog who replied, however, was clearly a native speaker. Yet his voice sounded familiar. As she had only ever met two native Furzish speakers in her whole life, she had little difficulty in pinning down the hedgehog in question.

58

It was Monsieur Espinon, who had been shipwrecked and rescued by her father just over a year ago. Quiller had been staying with them at the time, and she remembered how close the two of them had become. But why had Quiller not told her that Espinon was to visit the island? Indeed, why had Espinon taken a room at the inn, when he could have stayed far more comfortably at Quiller's house? Perhaps, if she listened, she would find out...

"I shall see you in the morning then," said Quiller, still in Furzish. "Shall we say... at nine o'clock? Mr Orbrey lives some considerable distance away."

"Yes, very well, nine o'clock," said Espinon. "But stay a moment, Quiller. I would talk with you."

"Yes? Is something the matter, Espinon?

"My dear Quiller, you can hardly be at a loss to know what it is I wish to discuss. The events of this evening did not inspire me with much confidence. I had certainly not expected the Customs Service to be waiting for us."

"Nor I," responded Quiller. "But I cannot see that this is any cause for your concern. Indeed, there were only two of them."

"What difference does that make?" said Espinon. "We may be as easily discovered by two hedgehogs as by two-and-twenty!"

"Two are more easily dealt with," said Quiller.

Hoglinda had to suppress a gasp of horror. The shooting tonight had already shown her just how far the smugglers would go, but to hear her own cousin speak this way was shocking.

"True," said Espinon, "but another time there may be more."

"Another time there may be none," said Quiller. "Indeed, that is the more likely. Customs officers are spread thinly over the island; they seldom come to the Back."

"Then why are they come tonight?" asked Espinon sharply. "Perhaps you have been betrayed."

"Espinon, that is most improbable. If the Customs Service had been informed of our landing, they would have sent a much larger force... But it's your own project you're thinking of, is it not? You really need have no fear on that count. I am quite sure your generosity has bought the silence of all involved. And, if any hedgehog *were* tempted to betray you, he must understand that, with the stakes so high, betrayal could not go unpunished - that he would be risking his life."

"Perhaps you are right," said Espinon. "I certainly hope so, for there is, indeed, a great deal at stake."

"Yes, I know it... Now, Espinon, if there is nothing that cannot wait till morning, I must take my leave of you. Hoglinda awaits my return and she will begin to worry."

"Your cousin does not know of your activities, I presume?" said Espinon.

"Well, she knows that I smuggle."

Hearing this last exchange, a whisker of suspicion passed through Hoglinda's mind. Did this mean that Quiller was engaged in *other* unlawful activities, besides smuggling? Even more serious than smuggling? Without further delay, she crept down the stairs, grabbed her lantern and then slipped out of the Hog's Head Inn. All her focus now had to be on getting home before Quiller did. Yet, as she hurried through the darkness, she could not stop thinking about the conversation she had just overheard. Why had Monsieur Espinon come back to the Isle of Needles? What was this project they spoke of? And what was Quiller's role in it?

Quiller arrived home a few minutes after Hoglinda; but it was just enough. She had by then changed out of her disguise and, though there was no time to put the clothes back, she had at least managed to hide them under her bed. When Quiller came through the front door, she appeared on the stairs in her dressing gown, holding a candlestick in one paw and stifling a yawn with the other.

"Oh!" exclaimed Quiller. "Were you gone to bed? Have I disturbed you? I fully expected to find you pacing up and down the parlour, anxiously awaiting my return."

"I am certainly glad to see you are come back safely," she responded.

"Well then," he said, "if you are not too sleepy, why don't you join me in the parlour? I shall tell you all."

Hoglinda followed Quiller into the parlour, hoping rather than expecting that he would give her a full and truthful account of the evening.

"You were well out of it, Hoglinda, I can assure you," he said, as he pulled off his boots to warm his feet by the fire. "It was a hard night. There were Customs officers about - though, thankfully, we had fair warning, for Mrs Tipps had not lit her usual candle. So we unloaded the cargo in Whiskercombe Bay. There, at least, the coast was clear."

61

"Whiskercombe Bay!" exclaimed Hoglinda. She was astonished, for the bay was surrounded by high chalk cliffs on every side. "So you must have had to leave the cargo on the beach then?"

"No, we dared not risk it. Tubby is hoisting it up on ropes as we speak. It may take all night, but that cannot be helped."

"Did you yourself meet any Customs officers?" she asked.

"Not I, thank goodness; by the time I came ashore, they were gone. But the shore party themselves were not so fortunate. I understand shots were fired, and it is likely that one of Mr Tubby's hedgehogs may have been recognized."

"Was anyone hurt?"

"Not on our side."

"And on the Preventives' side?" asked Hoglinda, thinking of poor Snoach, lying wounded in the room next to Monsieur Espinon.

"I neither know nor care - at least, I would not care if poor Ruffley had not been recognized. Now he will have to lie low for a while - at least until the heat is off. It will be hard on him, for he has a wife and five hoglets… Now, talking of hoglets, how are mine? Have they been asking for me?"

"Every day! When Mrs Brush told them you were expected back tonight, she had difficulty persuading them to bed."

Quiller smiled. "Well, then they may yet be awake. I'll go up and take a look."

With that, the cousins wished each other goodnight. Hoglinda went to bed but could not sleep, for she found herself turning over again and again the events of the evening. She could not forget the conversation she had overheard at the inn. But what could she do about it? *Should* she try to do anything about it? Over the course of the last year, she had grown very fond of her cousin, and there was no denying his good qualities. He was a devoted father and a generous employer. Perhaps she was wrong to be suspicious. Yet it was not in her nature to leave the matter alone.

The following morning, Quiller went out straight after breakfast on a business call. Shortly afterwards Mrs Brush went shopping with the hoglets, to buy some cloth for new clothes. Then, about half an hour later, Pinafore left with a basket of food for Ruffley, the hedgehog who was in hiding from the Customs Service. The coast was clear. Hoglinda made straight for Quiller's study. She first put back the old clothes she had worn the previous night. Then she set about searching the study for clues - just as she had done eight months earlier. This time, though it still pricked her conscience, her nerves were steadier; and she found the desk key immediately, for it was still hidden behind the clock on the mantelpiece, exactly where she had found it all those months before.

Picking up Quiller's journal, she examined the previous day's entry: he had noted down the times of high tide and moonset. But there was no mention of Monsieur Espinon - or, indeed, of anyone else involved in the smuggling run. So she turned her attention to his pile of papers. Among them were two letters from Espinon. The first had been written on the 6th of December - just over a month ago.

My dear Quiller, it read,

I trust this letter finds you well. You will remember my idea - which we discussed while at your uncle's house so many months ago. When I put this idea to others, on my return to Furze, I could find no one who would listen. But much has changed since then. I now at last have approval to draw up a detailed plan for them to consider. I therefore propose to make a further visit to the Isle of Needles and I should be very much obliged if you would lend me your assistance. If you agree, I suggest that we meet in Gruntsey on your next visit and return thence to the Isle of Needles together. I should mention that I have already written to several wine merchants in St Pricklier Port and propose to visit them while I am there. In this way, I believe I may attract as little attention as possible.

Now I have one more thing to ask of you and I am afraid it is no little thing. I know from my own experience the dangers of the Isle of Needles' south coast. In view of this, I believe it will be necessary to employ local pilots. If you will find for me four hedgehogs who are able and willing to act as pilots, I shall be enormously grateful. I believe every hedgehog has his price. You will, of course, be repaid any expense you may incur.

I need hardly add that discretion will be necessary at every stage.

I am ever your obedient servant,
Espinon

Hoglinda reached for Quiller's ledger and looked through all the payments made since the 6th of December. Three payments of £100 apiece stood out from the rest; for no other payments came anywhere near this. They were to a 'Mr O', a 'Mr B' and a 'Mr C' for goods or services unspecified. Could O, B and C be the pilots Espinon had asked for? They were only three, of course, but Quiller might still be looking for a fourth. Yet she could not believe a pilot would be paid that much. Pilots were employed to guide boats to shore where the approach was particularly difficult or dangerous; and they were highly valued for their local knowledge and expertise. But Mr Cutliss knew the local coast like the back of his paw and he had just taken the *Hogspur* all the way to Gruntsey and back for just £30.

Hoglinda unfolded the second letter, dated the 21st of December.

My dear Quiller, wrote Espinon,

Please do not apologise. Naturally, I regret that I shall not have the opportunity of meeting young Quillemina and Quillip, nor of seeing Miss Hoglinda again. But I quite understand why you will not be able to receive me in your home. Indeed, I am most grateful for the assistance you have been able to give me in this delicate matter. As for your progress on my behalf, I agree that it will be better that you do not commit the details to paper. I shall content myself therefore with waiting until we meet, when I may hear from you in person.

With regards to our meeting, I have booked my passage to Gruntsey. I expect to arrive by the 8th of January - wind and weather permitting - and shall leave word with my ship where I am to be found. She is called the 'Rapière' and will remain in port for seven or eight days at least. But perhaps I shall find you first.

I am ever your obedient servant,
Espinon

So here was confirmation - as if it were needed - that Quiller had deliberately sought to hide Espinon's presence from her. But why? She could not begin to fathom what it was all about. If only there were someone she could turn to for advice. She briefly considered writing to one of her father's friends but then dismissed the idea. She dared not write a letter, in case it fell into the paws of the Customs Service. Furthermore, it would be impossible to explain anything without revealing Quiller's and her own smuggling activities. The only safe course of action was to speak to someone who was just as guilty in the eyes of the law as they were. But nearly everyone she could think of was closely connected with Quiller in one way or another - Mrs Tipps, Captain Cutliss and Mr Tubby, Mrs Brush and Pinafore... There was just one hedgehog who, she believed, would feel no ties of loyalty to her cousin.

Hoglinda set off across the downs without delay and arrived at Bristlestone Mill shortly before noon. The mill was situated on the edge of the village, about a mile from the sea. It was a small, humble building made of stone rubble, its thatched roof in some need of repair. But there were signs of activity. Leaning against the front wall were three large sacks of flour; and the water wheel was in operation, turning noisily as the mill stream cascaded over it. Hoglinda knocked and waited nervously. The door was opened by Mr Snipwicke himself. He was in his shirtsleeves and there were specks of flour upon his waistcoat.

"Why, Miss Hoglinda!" he exclaimed, hastily brushing the flour away. "What a pleasant surprise!"

Hoglinda thought he looked more surprised than pleased at her unexpected appearance on his doorstep. At their last meeting - three months ago, they had not parted on the best of terms.

"I do hope I am not intruding, Mr Snipwicke. Perhaps you have company?"

"No, you find me all alone. Please, come in."

Stepping inside, Hoglinda found herself straightaway in the parlour, for there was no hallway. The room was small and plain, but she noticed it contained several items of surprisingly good furniture, which would not have been out of place in her father's house.

"Are you in Bristlestone on your cousin's business?" asked Snipwicke, as they sat down.

"Not exactly, Mr Snipwicke. My cousin knows nothing of my visit, but it is *concerning* my cousin that I am come. I would like your advice on... well, on a matter of some delicacy."

"Oh!" Snipwicke looked astonished. "I cannot imagine what could... Forgive me - please go on."

Hoglinda took a deep breath. "I fear my cousin is involved in some secret activity," she said, "something unlawful - that is, besides smuggling. Indeed, I heard him say that anyone who betrayed this secret would be risking his life."

"I see. That must have been a shock for you. But you must understand, Miss Hoglinda, that smuggling is no game. Informers are dealt with roughly. Some even pay for their disloyalty with their lives."

Hoglinda stared at Snipwicke, little shivers creeping down her spines. "Do you mean my cousin has... that you have...?"

"No, Miss Hoglinda, I have never killed anyone - neither has Quiller, as far as I know. And I hope I never shall."

Hoglinda was scarcely reassured by this reply. She felt she had been a fool to come. Snipwicke was Quiller's rival, but that was no reason to suppose he was essentially any different to Quiller - any better than him.

"I should go," she said, getting up hastily. "I really don't know what I was thinking of, coming here..."

"I do," said Snipwicke. "You were thinking that your cousin and I are not the best of friends; that you could not go to the authorities and dared not confide in any of Quiller's circle. You were thinking that I was the only hedgehog in these parts to whom you could safely turn."

"And was I right?" asked Hoglinda.

"Yes, you were," said Snipwicke. He smiled reassuringly.

Hoglinda reflected for a moment. She knew little of Snipwicke's character. It seemed most unlikely that he would repeat her suspicions to Quiller; but might he instead try to use this information *against* him? Whatever Quiller's secret was, he was still her cousin. She looked Snipwicke in the eye. She could find no hint of malice in his expression or, indeed, in anything he had said. She sat down again.

"Now, Miss Hoglinda," said Snipwicke. "Why don't you tell me exactly what it is that has caused you so much concern?"

Hoglinda proceeded to relate the events of the previous evening. She explained that Espinon had first become known to her family when he had been shipwrecked off the island. She then told Snipwicke about the contents of the letters she had just found and the payments recorded in Quiller's ledger. Of course, it was embarrassing to admit that she had been going through her cousin's private papers and eavesdropping on his conversations, but that could not be helped. If Snipwicke disapproved, at least he did not show it.

"So what do you reckon this plan might be?" he asked.

"I really have no idea, for I could make neither head nor tail of their conversation. That is the problem, Mr Snipwicke: I am all at sea."

"But you must surely have some suspicion in your mind - else you would not be come all this way to seek my advice."

"You think I am making something out of nothing?" asked Hoglinda.

"Not at all. Drawing up a detailed plan for others' approval sounds strangely formal. And, if your cousin is paying these pilots £100 each as you suspect, this can be no ordinary smuggling run. Why, a hedgehog could live fairly comfortably on that sum for an entire year!"

Hoglinda did not altogether agree. Her own allowance of £120 was just pin money. If she had had to pay for her food and lodging out of it, as well as her clothes, she would have found it most unsatisfactory; but she did not say so, of course. She was well aware that most of the smugglers she knew would consider £100 a very large sum indeed.

"Mr Snipwicke," she said, "since you clearly share my suspicions, may I ask what *you* think my cousin is about?"

Snipwicke smiled but would not be drawn. "First tell me more about Monsieur Espinon," he said, going off on another tack altogether. "When he was staying at your father's house, did he explain what he had been doing on board a Furzish warship?"

"Oh, it wasn't a warship - only a naval cutter," explained Hoglinda. "You see, navies use cutters to carry personnel, messages and the like. This particular cutter was on a coastal patrol out of Pawdeaux and bound for Le Hogre, when the storm blew her off course. As for Monsieur Espinon, he was on his way to visit an associate in Le Hogre on a matter of business."

"What kind of business?"

"I do not know for certain but I imagine it was in connection with his vineyards in Pawdeaux."

"So Monsieur Espinon is in the wine business!" exclaimed Snipwicke. "Well then, that makes a *big* difference. It is no great stretch from wine grower to wine merchant, nor from merchant to smuggler. You know, I begin to think this business with Quiller may turn out to be nothing more than a smuggling venture after all... And yet..." Snipwicke stroked the fur on his chin, as he gave the matter some thought. "And yet I wonder how he obtained his berth on the navy cutter, if he was not travelling on navy business. Were there any other passengers on board?"

"No, just Monsieur Espinon, but I believe Lieutenant Oursin is a friend of his."

"I see. So perhaps Oursin was just doing a friend a favour. But that still leaves the matter of the payments to explain. Perhaps we were mistaken about them. They may be nothing to do with Espinon after all."

"But, Mr Snipwicke, the payments are not the only loose end - they are not the only thing that cannot be explained away. You are forgetting that Quiller has deliberately concealed Monsieur Espinon's presence from me."

"Ah yes, of course... Hmm... I suppose nothing happened at your father's house to cause any awkwardness or ill-feeling between you and Monsieur Espinon?"

"No, we all got on very well. My father and I both liked Monsieur Espinon, and I believe he liked us; but I must confess that, after a time, it seemed always to be Quiller he sought out. I should add that I believe this was out of a positive preference for Quiller's company rather than any dislike of mine! Certainly at no point did he seek to avoid me - or have any reason to do so."

"And what do you think was the basis of this close friendship with Quiller? Did they seem to have much in common?"

"Not particularly, that I could tell. But the thing that really struck me was just how sudden this closeness between them was. I can pinpoint the exact occasion. It was almost overnight, you might say. From then on, they were always wandering off alone together whenever we were out. But what they discussed, I cannot say."

"More's the pity," said Snipwicke. "But what of earlier on - before he developed this preference for Quiller's company? What were you able to learn about him then?"

"Not much, I am afraid. Most of our conversations were on the subject of art. Monsieur Espinon likes to paint when he has the time."

"Indeed!" exclaimed Snipwicke. "Well, that seems an innocent enough occupation..." He smiled. "Are you an artist yourself, Miss Hoglinda?"

"Oh, no, I would not call myself that! But I am certainly fond of drawing and painting, and I was only too pleased to show him the best viewpoints. Not that he always followed my suggestions. He seemed always to have a very clear idea as to what interested him and what did not. It was odd, really, for he made so many sketches that he left himself no time to paint from them - and the sketches were so fine - so very detailed."

"I see. And do you remember which views he sketched?"

"Yes, I think so. Let me see... The view he seemed most taken by was Brambling Harbour. He certainly sketched it from every possible angle! He also drew Scratchdown Bay, the road north into Brambling, and the view along the top of Brambling Down, looking east and west along the road."

Snipwicke frowned and, getting up from his chair, began to pace up and down in an agitated manner.

"What is it, Mr Snipwicke? What have I said?"

Snipwicke sat down again and looked at her gravely. "I think we may be getting somewhere after all. But you will not like what I have to say."

Hoglinda bristled. "And what might that be?"

"I suspect that Monsieur Espinon may be a Furzish spy."

"A spy!" exclaimed Hoglinda, who did not like it at all. "And are you also suggesting that my cousin is a traitor?"

"Consider this," said Snipwicke, ignoring her last point. "The Furzish are our traditional enemies. The Furzish Navy is known to be carrying weapons to the rebels in our western colonies, and it surely cannot be long before war breaks out between our two countries again. Now, Espinon was the sole passenger on board a cutter of the Furzish Navy, and we have only his word for it that he was not engaged on navy or other government business. When he was staying at your father's house, he made detailed sketches of our island: all of those sketches were of roads and landing places. Since then, he has asked your cousin to recruit four pilots on his behalf, which means that he must be planning some sort of landing, involving at least four vessels. And now he is returned to the island in secret in order to draw up a detailed plan for his colleagues to consider. Perhaps also to meet those pilots who are to be so well paid. Now, when you put all of this together, it can surely only mean one thing. The Furzish are planning an invasion of the Isle of Needles."

Hoglinda was stunned. "No, I cannot believe it!" she exclaimed. "I *will* not. My cousin may have his faults, but he is no traitor. The Isle of Needles is his home, as much as it is yours or mine. What possible motive could he have to do such a thing?"

"I imagine he will be paid for his efforts."

"No, Mr Snipwicke, you are on completely the wrong tack," said Hoglinda crossly. "Espinon's letter said he would be reimbursed for any expenses, but there was no mention of payment. Indeed, Quiller has no need of it - he lives very comfortably as it is."

"Where there is no need, there may still be greed," said Snipwicke. "But you may be right - he may have some motive other than money."

"I said no such thing!" protested Hoglinda, indignantly. "You are twisting my words, Mr Snipwicke. Perhaps we should examine *your* motives. You hate my cousin. You would love to see him out of the way."

"Let us remember, Miss Hoglinda," said Snipwicke angrily, "that it was *you* who came to see *me* on this matter."

Hoglinda felt the tears welling up. She had to leave before she made an exhibition of herself. She made for the door, but Snipwicke barred her way.

"I want to go," she said quietly. "Kindly get out of my way."

"Not until you have heard me out," said Snipwicke. He looked at her sternly but she would not meet his eye. "You are right that we do not know Quiller's motive. Indeed, we have no hard proof against him - or against Monsieur Espinon, for that matter. The evidence in this case is purely circumstantial. But I can see no other explanation that fits all the facts, as we know them. Moreover, if I am right - if Monsieur Espinon is indeed a spy, then Quiller is implicated and the security of the nation is at stake. We *cannot* ignore this."

Hoglinda stared at her feet, the wind taken out of her sails. "I will not see my cousin hang," she insisted, as a solitary tear fell upon her shoe.

"It need not come to that," said Snipwicke, more gently now.

Hoglinda looked up. "How so?"

"Well, as I said, the evidence is circumstantial. Before anything can be done, we need proof. When we have it, we will confront Quiller with it. We can then give him a choice - exile or face the law."

"You would have him banished from his own country?"

"If he has betrayed his country, he deserves no less."

"But what of Quillemina and Quillip?" said Hoglinda. "They have harmed no one."

"I am sorry," said Snipwicke. "Truly I am. I wish there were some other way, but there is not."

Snipwicke looked at her with such an expression of sympathy that she believed him. It did not lessen her pain, but she began to believe that this was a hedgehog in whom she could place her trust. Yet still she hesitated. Quiller was her cousin. He had taken her into his home. He had been kind to her, and she was very fond of him. But what if Snipwicke was right? If the Isle of Needles were invaded and she had not lifted a paw to prevent it, how could she live with herself then? She, an admiral's daughter!

"Very well, Mr Snipwicke," she said, pulling herself together at last and returning to her seat. "How do you propose that we find this evidence?"

When Hoglinda returned home that afternoon, Quiller was still out. The hoglets were playing in the parlour, and Pinafore and Mrs Brush were busy preparing dinner in the kitchen. Hoglinda went upstairs, opened and shut her bedroom door noisily without entering, and then crept over to Quiller's room. This time she shut the door very gently behind her. Then she began her search. It ought not to take long, she thought, for there was just a chest-of-drawers and a small closet to go through. Yet, for a moment, she allowed her attention to be distracted by the painting above the chest-of-drawers. It was a portrait of Quiller's late wife, the beautiful and tragic Hedgrietta, who had died when Quillip was barely out of his cradle. A pang of guilt shot through Hoglinda's heart. Had Quiller not suffered enough already? Then she heard Snipwicke's voice in her head, reminding her that the security of the nation was at stake.

Rummaging through the chest-of-drawers, Hoglinda found a bundle of letters tied together with a blue ribbon. When she discovered they were from Hedgrietta, she hastily retied the ribbon and returned them to the drawer. There was just one other letter there, that was not part of the bundle. It was from her own father, Admiral Hoglander, and concerned Hedgerietta's brother, Hedginald. Hedginald had gone to live in the colonies a number of years ago - the very colonies where the admiral was now fighting to put down a rebellion.

My dear Quiller, it read.

I hope this letter finds you all well. Quillemina and Quillip will, I am sure, have grown a great deal since last I saw them. I fear I shall scarcely recognize them when I return! I trust that Hoglinda has been useful to you and not a nuisance. She certainly writes to me that she is busy and happy. Indeed, I believe these months with you have done her a great deal of good and I am most grateful to you for it.

But it is regarding a less happy matter that I write to you, for I have received news that your brother-in-law, Hedginald, has been taken prisoner. I should explain that he was fighting for the rebels - I do not know if this is news to you - but I understand that he has always behaved openly and honourably. And, though he and I fight on opposite sides, rest assured that I am doing what I can to ensure he is comfortable.

Your affectionate
Uncle Hoglander

Hoglinda stared at the letter. Was this Quiller's motive? She felt it must be. Quiller had made it clear more than once that he expected the rebels to win. Now she believed it was more than an expectation - it was his wish. No doubt Hedginald had won him over to the rebels' cause. Quiller and Hedginald had been good friends even before Quiller's marriage to Hedgrietta. Hoglinda remembered meeting Hedginald once, at the wedding. She had been just a hoglet then, but he had had a way of charming everyone, whatever their age. Then he had gone off to live in the colonies. Now, it seemed, he had turned his back on the Bristlish Crown - and Quiller had done the same. Yet it was not at all the same! Hedginald had been honest about his sympathies; he had fought openly for his adopted country's independence. Quiller, so it seemed, had been dishonest and plotted secretly against Great Bristlin - which was still his country, whether he liked it or not.

Hoglinda's reflections were interrupted by voices in the hallway. It was Mrs Brush... and Quiller! Hoglinda quickly returned the letter to the chest-of-drawers and then made for the door, but it was too late. There were footsteps on the stairs. She dived under the bed. A moment later, Quiller walked into the room. Striding over to the bedside table, he poured some water into the bowl, washed his face and paws and then sat down heavily on the bed. Hoglinda tried hard to control her breathing, fearing he would hear her. Then there was a knock at the door.

"Yes?" said Quiller.

The door opened: it was Mrs Brush, who was out of breath and sounded worried.

"You've got a visitor, sir. 'Tes the Customs officer!"

"Mr Gimlet!" exclaimed Quiller. "Did he say what he wanted?"

"No, sir, but he ded say t'was both you and Miss Hoglinda he was aater."

"*Both* of us? Heavens! Oh, I should never have involved Hoglinda in any of this. What will her father say? - Mrs Brush, do you know where she is?"

"She come upstairs, sir, about ten minutes ago. I suppose she must be in her room."

Mrs Brush and Quiller left the room together. Then, not finding Hoglinda upstairs, they went down again - Quiller to the parlour to meet Mr Gimlet and Mrs Brush to the kitchen to attend to dinner. Hoglinda now came out from under the bed and crept down the stairs. She had no wish to meet Mr Gimlet again. Last night she had been worried he would recognize her from when they had met previously at her father's house. Now she was afraid he would recognize her as young Hoggin from the Hog's Head Inn. Taking her cloak, she slipped out the back way into the garden.

"Oh, there you be ma'am!" It was Pinafore, who had come out to empty a bucket. "We was wonderen' where you got to. You've a visitor waiten' for you in the parlour, wi' Mr Quiller."

Hoglinda turned round reluctantly. There was no escaping now. As she drew closer, Pinafore whispered in her ear: "Don't be alarmed, ma'am, but 'tes Mr Gimlet... the Preventive officer."

Hoglinda pretended to be surprised. "Mr Gimlet!" she exclaimed - also in a whisper. "Is it about last night?"

"Sorry, ma'am, but I don't rightly know."

Hoglinda shrugged her shoulders and went indoors to the parlour.

"Ah Hoglinda, there you are!" said Quiller. "This is Mr Gimlet from the Customs Service. Mr Gimlet, may I present my cousin, Hoglinda?"

Rising from his seat, Gimlet stared at her, with an unnerving smile. "Ma'am," he said, with a little bow. "I believe we have met before, have we not?"

"Why, yes, of course," she said, a little stiffly. "It was at my father's house, a year or so ago."

"Oh, is it as long ago as that?" responded Gimlet. "Why it feels like only yesterday!"

Hoglinda gulped. Was he playing with her? She sat down and forced herself to look him directly in the eye. "Mr Gimlet, to what do we owe the pleasure of your visit today?"

Looking rather furtive, Gimlet shut the door behind him, before returning to his chair. "The matter concerning which I am come to you today," he said gravely, "is of national importance, and I must insist upon your absolute secrecy - you must not breathe a word of this to anyone. Do I have your word upon that?"

Hoglinda was puzzled but greatly relieved, for she now realized that he had *not* recognized her from yesterday - it had been merely a manner of speech. Indeed, his visit seemed to have nothing to do with the events of yesterday evening at all. He had clearly come in friendship - not to arrest them.

"Yes, of course, Mr Gimlet," she said, "so long as there is no harm in it."

Quiller nodded his agreement.

"Thank you, Miss Hoglinda, Mr Quiller." Gimlet leant forward in his chair and then continued in a confidential tone. "I am afraid the government has received intelligence of a most alarming nature. The Furzish are negotiating a secret treaty with the rebels in our colonies. It is very likely the Furzish will soon recognize the colonies' independence. And, though they have not yet declared war upon Great Bristlin, they are even now preparing an invasion of the Isle of Needles."

Hoglinda managed to look astonished. Indeed, she *was* astonished - to be receiving this confirmation of Snipwicke's suspicions, so soon and from such a source. Her first thought was that Snipwicke must have betrayed her confidence and gone to the authorities after all. But there could hardly have been enough time for that. Moreover, this reference to a secret treaty was new. She glanced at Quiller to see how he reacted and was just in time to see him shift awkwardly in his chair. The look of discomfort on his face was unmistakeable to one who knew what she knew. But a moment later it was gone. She hoped that Gimlet had not noticed it.

"That is grave news," said Quiller. "Grave news indeed. But what has it to do with the Customs Service - and why do you entrust this intelligence to us?"

"Because there are said to be local smugglers in the pay of the Furzish, who are to pilot their ships to shore for them. Now, there are several possible landing places, including Hog's Head Bay, and we all know that smugglers are as common here as elsewhere on the island... So I am come to ask whether you have heard or seen anything unusual. You might, for instance, know of a hedgehog who has suddenly come into a great deal of money... more money than could be explained by an ordinary smuggling run. Let us say - "

"This is hardly likely," interrupted Hoglinda, pretending to be offended. "My cousin and I do not mix in such circles."

"Oh, that was not at all what I meant!" said Gimlet hastily. "Indeed, had I thought *that,* I would not be here. But, in other times I would have sought the assistance of your father, Miss Hoglinda. So, in his absence, I feel I can scarcely do better than consult his daughter and his nephew."

"Yet I am still unsure how we may help you," said Hoglinda.

"I ask only that you keep your ears pricked - rumours spread quickly in a place such as this - and, if you should hear anything - anything suspicious in any way, that you contact me at once."

"But how certain are you of this information?" asked Quiller. "What is its source?" He spoke as though this were the most reasonable question in the world.

"That, I'm afraid, I cannot say, Mr Quiller. Such information is a closely guarded secret. I know only that the report is considered to be completely reliable, but that we can expect no further reports from that source."

"Well then, we shall try to find out what we can for you," said Quiller, "though I fear it will not be much."

"Thank you," said Gimlet. "I am most grateful."

"Not at all," said Quiller, smiling a little unnaturally. "Don't mention it. Now, can I tempt you to a glass of wine?"

Gimlet stayed for dinner. He clearly enjoyed associating with the gentry and regarded them as above suspicion. And, though Hoglinda was constantly afraid he would ask Quiller where he got his wine from, he thankfully showed no curiosity on that count. Quite what Quiller meant by inviting him to dinner, she was unsure; but he seemed anxious to be friendly with Gimlet and, every now and then,

would gently probe for more information about the Furzish invasion plan. Unsurprisingly, Gimlet was either unwilling or unable to tell them any more.

After dinner, as soon as Mr Gimlet had gone, Quiller went out. He claimed he was going to visit Ruffley, the smuggler who was in hiding from the Customs Service; Hoglinda did not believe a word of it. About five minutes after he had left, she left, too, and headed back to the Hog's Head Inn, wearing the same masculine clothes that she had worn the previous night.

The inn was even busier than on her first visit. Clearly news had got out that Mrs Tipps had restocked her 'cellar' the previous evening. When Hoglinda arrived, Mrs Tipps was busy fetching more wine, so Hoglinda was able to slip upstairs without being spotted by her. The door to Espinon's room was shut and a light showed under it. All the other rooms were unoccupied; presumably Snoach had been taken home - where he would no doubt receive more constant and devoted attention. Hoglinda slipped into the room next to Espinon's and, closing the door gently behind her, put her ear to the wall.

There were voices - Espinon's and Quiller's voices, just as she had expected. She thought Quiller sounded a little defensive.

"I can assure you," she heard him say, "they did not get this information from here. I said nothing of a treaty to Orbrey or

Buckthorn - nor even to Cutliss. So it could not have been any of them. Besides, Gimlet clearly viewed me as above suspicion: that would hardly be the case if the informant were one of my associates."

"Well, perhaps you may be right about that," said Espinon, "in which case, *you* may breathe easier, but not I. If the informant is not here on the Isle of Needles, then he must be close to the Furzish government. That means we have a Bristlish spy in our midst, and our situation is a great deal more serious than I thought."

"So what will you do now?" asked Quiller. "I suppose you must abandon your plan."

"Well, yes, as things stand, it would be unwise to pursue it. I'm afraid that means the pilots you've engaged will receive no further payment. I hope that will not present you with any difficulty."

"Oh, I shouldn't think so. After all, you are under no obligation to go through with your plan."

"No, that is true. Still, perhaps we shall return to it at a later date... Indeed, I think it very likely... If we do, may I rely upon your assistance once more?"

"Why, yes," said Quiller. "But, of course, at a later date, you may wish to use another landing place - somewhere other than the Isle of Needles, as by then the circumstances may be very different. If this does turn out to be the case, I will quite understand."

"What circumstances do you speak of?" asked Espinon.

"Well, at present, your forces could expect to land on the Isle of Needles virtually unopposed - as you know. There might not even be a single shot fired. But, following their discovery of your invasion plan, the Bristlish government may well decide to strengthen the island's defences. And it would make no sense for you to land on the Isle of Needles if it were better defended than the mainland."

"I am not sure I agree," said Espinon. "After so many months of preparation, we should not throw away our plan so lightly. Think what we have achieved: we have a detailed map of the island, sketches of our landing sites and our routes inland; we have the three pilots you have recruited to bring us safely to shore. Neither should we forget why I chose the Isle of Needles in the first place - because it is an island. Here we may recover and reorganize, before we prepare for the main invasion. We will have all the resources we need - a military depot, stores of corn for our soldiers and even a military hospital, should we suffer any casualties. No, I believe the Isle of Needles would have to be a great deal better defended than it is now before it would make sense to look elsewhere."

"Perhaps you are right," said Quiller, "but, even so, there must be a point at which you would prefer to look for alternatives."

"Why, yes, of course," said Espinon. "But, look here, Quiller, you begin to sound as though you would *prefer* us to look elsewhere!"

"No," said Quiller, thoughtfully, "I only prefer to avoid unnecessary bloodshed - on both sides, for the hedgehogs who live upon this island are not only my neighbours, many of them are also my friends."

"Yes, of course, I understand that," said Espinon. "I also would like to avoid unnecessary bloodshed. Rest assured, Quiller, we shall make the decision as best we can, based upon the information we have available to us at the time. Indeed, if *you* would undertake to keep us informed, I think that would answer very nicely."

"Me!" exclaimed Quiller.

"Yes. Who better?"

"But I am no soldier. I am ill qualified to report on military matters."

"Nonsense. I am not asking you for an assessment - only the facts. Such as the arrival of additional troops on the island... or the construction of new fortifications."

"And how would I get this information to you?"

"There is a hedgehog in Gruntsey who reports to us anything of interest that can be picked up from the ships visiting St Pricklier Port. As soon as you have any information to communicate, sail to Gruntsey and wait to be contacted. Our hedgehog knows all the comings and goings and, when the *Hogspur* arrives, will know about it and seek you out. That way you need entrust nothing to paper."

"How will I know him?"

"*She* will know you."

There was a slight pause in the conversation. "Very well," said Quiller at last. "I will do as you ask."

"My dear fellow!" said Espinon with obvious delight. "Thank you! Now I have just one more thing to ask of you. I must, of course, return to Furze as soon as possible. Indeed, there is no time to be lost. The spy who has betrayed my country must be identified and caught before it is too late. Luckily, the ship that brought me from Furze will still be in St Pricklier Port - for I was assured she would not sail before the 15th of January. If you can get me to Gruntsey before then, I can sail home in her."

"But, Espinon, I'm afraid you may already be too late to catch this spy. Gimlet said they could expect no further information from their source. That suggests the spy is no longer in place."

"Perhaps it does. But other secrets may have been betrayed besides this one. Until we can at least identify the spy, we shall have no means of knowing what or how much damage has been done."

"No, I suppose not," conceded Quiller. "Well then, I shall, of course, speak to Cutliss first thing tomorrow morning. But I should warn you, you may have to wait a day or two before the *Hogspur* is ready to sail. She is now moored in Hogmouth Harbour on the north coast and the crew has been dispersed. With a fair wind, we should be able to get you to Gruntsey in time, but I'm afraid there is no guarantee... I say 'we' but, in fact, I shall not be able to accompany you on this occasion. I have business here I must attend to."

"Of course, I quite understand. My passage to Gruntsey is all I ask."

Here the conversation sounded as though it was coming to an end. It was time for Hoglinda to leave. Once again, she high-tailed it out of the Hog's Head Inn ahead of her cousin and, dashing home, got there just before him.

Chapter Eight
12th January 1778

The following morning, Hoglinda and Snipwicke met at the causeway, as they had arranged to do when she had visited him the previous day. Hoglinda listened impatiently while Snipwicke told her his news, for she was bursting with her own.

"I'm glad to say I have made some progress," said Snipwicke, with an air of quiet satisfaction. "One of my customers has a cousin in Blackfang village, who says that Quiller and another hedgehog, with a Furzish accent, called upon a neighbour of his yesterday. A certain Mr Orbrey, just as we expected! Apparently, Orbrey is an experienced sailor, who's worked in the Trade for many years. Yet he's always struggled to make ends meet, for he has a large family to feed. Recently, however, he has been seen splashing his money about a fair bit. Now, it's said that Orbrey knows his stretch of coast like the back of his paw. And it seems to me that it wouldn't be a bad stretch of coast for an invading force. In fact, so long as you have the help of an experienced pilot - such as Orbrey - I would say Curle Bay is an obvious landing place. The invaders can come off the beach through Blackfang Chine, follow the road to Curle village and then it's straight

84

on to Nippert... So there you have it, Miss Hoglinda! I believe we have discovered the first of Espinon's pilots: Orbrey is our 'Mr O'. Of course, the others will not be so easy to identify, but I would be very much surprised if Cutliss were not Mr C."

"He is!" said Hoglinda eagerly, "and the third pilot is called Buckthorn."

"Oh!" said Snipwicke, who was suitably astonished. "Well, this is excellent news! What else were you able to find out?"

Hoglinda now went on to explain how everything had changed since they had spoken the previous day. "So you see," she said, as she finished, "Monsieur Espinon now intends to cut short his visit and may leave as early as tomorrow. I think it very likely he will meet this other hedgehog in St Pricklier Port, whoever she may be, in order to explain what has happened and to set up this new arrangement between her and Quiller."

"Yes, that does seem likely," agreed Snipwicke. He stroked his chin thoughtfully. "Perhaps this will give me the opportunity to identify her, this er... well, let us call her 'Madame X' - as long as I am able to reach Gruntsey ahead of their meeting. Thankfully the *Sea Urchin* - my little lugger – she won't take nearly so long to make ready as the *Hogspur* will. I have her beached nearby and she requires just a skipper and two crew to sail her... The only difficulty will be persuading my crew to make the trip, as we are only recently returned from our last run. We have unfortunately sold very little of our cargo so far."

"Oh!" said Hoglinda. She knew enough of smuggling by now to understand that many smugglers lived paw-to-mouth: the sale of contraband from one run was often needed to pay the expenses of the next. But what was a problem for Snipwicke, was no problem for Hoglinda. "Please don't worry about financing this trip, Mr Snipwicke," she said. "I had, of course, assumed that I would pay for my passage. Rest assured that I shall make it worth everyone's while."

"Your passage!" exclaimed Snipwicke. "But surely you do not expect to come to Gruntsey yourself! Why would you want to? You must know the risks. Hedgehogs are lost at sea every year."

"That does not prevent *you* from setting sail," said Hoglinda.

"I go to sea, Miss Hoglinda, because that is how I earn my living - the Mill scarcely pays for itself. But there is no need at all for you to come on this trip. To be frank, there's little room in my boat for passengers – it would be very cramped indeed; and it will be far easier for me to make my enquiries without you. I am a regular visitor and well-known as a trader. What reason could *you* give for your presence? Indeed, how would you explain your absence to Quiller?"

"Oh, that is easy!" said Hoglinda dismissively. "I shall just tell him my father's steward has written to me asking for my assistance. I'll say it's on a private matter of some urgency, concerning my father's estate; and that I must therefore go home to Brambling for a few days. As for how I shall explain my presence to the Gruntsey islanders - if they should ask - I will simply say that I am travelling for pleasure. Indeed, there is some truth in that," she added, smiling, "for I confess I do feel a *little* excited at the thought of visiting Gruntsey."

Snipwicke looked stern. "This will be no pleasure trip, Miss Hoglinda. At best your presence would be a distraction. At worst - "

"Not so!" interrupted Hoglinda. "You have never set eyes on Monsieur Espinon. How will you recognize him without me?"

"He hasn't left the Isle of Needles yet, Miss Hoglinda: you can point him out here."

Hoglinda hesitated for a moment, as she struggled to find another reason why Snipwicke should take her with him. "Do you speak Furzish?" she asked at last.

"I get by."

"So you are not fluent then!" said Hoglinda triumphantly. "Well, Mr Snipwicke, I am! It is thanks to my fluency that I have been able to learn so much already about this matter. And, in Gruntsey, it will be all the more important to have someone present who speaks Furzish well. After all, it is not merely Monsieur Espinon's language, but the language of the Gruntsey islanders, too. Indeed, it is very probable that your 'Madame X' will herself be a Furzish speaker."

Snipwicke hesitated. Though he began to see she had a point and might be useful after all, he still did not much like the idea of taking her with him. "Well," he said at last, "perhaps you should come - but not unaccompanied. Do you have your maid with you?"

"No, Quiller's maid, Pinafore, serves me as well as him. But perhaps you could suggest someone suitable. I will, of course, pay her generously."

"I am sure you will," said Snipwicke wryly. There was something strangely annoying about Hoglinda's ability to throw money at every problem. Yet he had to admit there was more to her than her money. She was clever and brave - and stubborn, too.

Part 2
Chapter Nine
13th January 1778

Hoglinda and Snipwicke agreed to meet at noon the next day and depart with the outgoing tide. In the meantime, Snipwicke made the necessary arrangements with his crew. And Hoglinda wrote herself a letter, purporting to be from her father's steward and urging her to come home as soon as possible. Opening the letter in front of Quiller, she read it silently to herself, as though for the first time. She then assumed a look of concern, explained the contents of the letter to her cousin and told him she must return to Brambling the very next morning. When Quiller offered to accompany her, she thanked him but, of course, refused; she assured him that she could manage very well on her own.

The following morning, Hoglinda rose with the sun and arrived at Bristlestone Mill earlier than arranged, only to find Snipwicke out. She then spent an impatient half hour pacing up and down, wondering whether he had changed his mind. But he appeared at noon, just as agreed. With him was another hedgehog who, Hoglinda assumed, must be her new maid.

"Mr Snipwicke, you are come at last!" she said.

"Oh, have you been waiting long, Miss Hoglinda?" he asked, amused by her eagerness. "Allow me to present to you my sister, Spinet."

"Your sister!" exclaimed Hoglinda, who was surprised and somewhat concerned that Snipwicke would choose to involve his family in her affairs. Had he told Spinet about Quiller, she wondered? "I am very pleased to meet you, Miss Spinet," she said, forcing a smile. "Are you come to see your brother off?"

"Why no, Miss Hoglinda! I am to come with you. When Snipwicke told me you would be travelling without a maid, it occurred to me I could be of some assistance. The family I work for up at Northclaw Manor - I am a governess, you see - they are away at present. So, for a short while, I am free to do exactly as I please." She smiled and then added, "I believe a visit to Gruntsey would please me a great deal."

"It would?" said Hoglinda, trying to cover her confusion. Though Snipwicke and Spinet were not her social equals, this arrangement seemed highly improper to her. Spinet was a governess, not a servant.

Snipwicke noticed her hesitation, but misunderstood it. "Spinet will be a useful addition to our party, Miss Hoglinda," he said. "She knows Gruntsey well, and you can rely upon her discretion."

"I am sure I can," said Hoglinda. "But it hardly seems right... "

"Oh, I see what you are thinking," said Spinet, finally guessing the cause of Hoglinda's discomfort. "Please do not concern yourself on my account. I am not offering to be your maid - merely your travelling companion."

"Why, yes, of course," said Hoglinda, as though the thought would never have occurred to her. She was, in fact, deeply embarrassed by her mistake and did her best to cover it up. "It was merely that... Well, I confess I am a little surprised your brother would let you take such a risk, Miss Spinet. He was very reluctant to let *me* go with him. Were you not, Mr Snipwicke?"

"I was reluctant in both cases, Miss Hoglinda; but Spinet can be just as persuasive as you. She has reminded me that our father took her across to Gruntsey several times."

With the matter now settled between them, the three hedgehogs made their way down to the coast. Following the stream down from Bristlestone Mill, they descended directly into Gorse Chine. This was one of a series of valleys along the south coast of the Isle of Needles,

carved through the soft cliffs by downland streams. It and the other chines were often used by smugglers, for they provided easy access to the beach - hidden away from prying eyes.

The trees in Gorse Chine grew tall and upright - not at all like the wind-blown trees up on the cliff tops. But, as the chine descended towards the coast, its steep sides gradually fell away and trees were replaced by scrub. When the sea came into view, they were met by a brisk wind.

Walking out onto Bristlestone Bay, Hoglinda had her first sight of Snipwicke's boat, the *Sea Urchin*; she had a flat-bottomed hull and had been pulled up onto the beach by her two crew, who were now waiting beside her. Hoglinda was a little shocked. Though the *Sea Urchin* was a lugger, like the *Hogspur*, the similarity ended there. She had never imagined the *Sea Urchin* would be quite so small. Could it really be safe for the five of them to cross the Channel in her? She was about to say something about this to Snipwicke but then thought better of it. He had warned her the *Sea Urchin* had little room for passengers. It had been her own choice to come; and, of course, Spinet was only coming as her companion. Yet she took comfort from Spinet's presence. If Snipwicke had thought it truly too dangerous, he would never have let *her* come along.

The two crew, Rip and Tar, came forward to meet them. They greeted Snipwicke and Spinet with obvious warmth. They had apparently all known each other since Snipwicke and Spinet were hoglets; Rip and Tar had then crewed the *Sea Urchin* for their father. However, when they were introduced to Hoglinda, a note of suspicion entered their voices. They touched their paws to their hats respectfully enough, but there was a coolness in their manner, which did not escape her. She assumed it must be because she was Quiller's cousin: the loyalty and admiration which he inspired in his own part of the island was apparently not shared here.

Snipwicke, Rip and Tar dragged the *Sea Urchin* down to the water's edge and then helped Hoglinda and Spinet climb aboard. Once all were safely in, they hoisted the mizzensail. Then they guided the *Sea Urchin* gently between the rocky ledges which made this stretch of coast so dangerous - but which Snipwicke and his crew, thankfully, knew so well. Once beyond the ledges, they unfurled the mainsail. Hoglinda felt a small jolt as it caught the wind. A tingle of excitement ran down her spines at the thought of Gruntsey, St Pricklier Port and its bustling quayside. But, when she turned back to watch the shore recede into the distance, it was her own island which absorbed her attention. The whole of the south-west coast was visible now. Bathed in the low winter sun, the cliffs of Bristlestone Bay appeared a rich ochre colour, while the chalk cliffs around Hog's Head Bay were a startling white in comparison. Beyond this, rising precariously from the sea and marking the westernmost point of the island, were the famous Needles Rocks - the chalk stacks which gave the Isle of Needles its name.

Snipwicke took little notice of this familiar scene. Taking a bearing, he marked their position on his chart. Then he got the crew to run out the log-line, while he turned a sandglass, to calculate their speed. Rip counted the knots in the line as it ran out behind the boat. One...two...three...four knots. The sand had run through. Snipwicke noted down the number in his log book, together with their direction of travel and the time of day. This exercise would then be repeated on the hour every hour to ensure they remained on course.

Hoglinda's thoughts had meanwhile taken a philosophical turn, as she watched her island grow smaller and smaller, until eventually it disappeared from view altogether. When all around them was only the sea, with no land in sight, she reflected how immense the world must

be. She remembered the globe in her father's house and thought of all the lands that lay beyond the ocean and of all the hedgehogs who lived in those lands. She remembered her father's tales of his life at sea and thought of all the wonderful places he had been to. Somehow it made her own island and her own life seem small and unimportant; and, for all her present excitement, she felt a little sad.

Snipwicke noticed her downcast expression. "I do hope you are not feeling homesick, Miss Hoglinda? And so early in our voyage!"

"Quite the reverse, I assure you! I was just thinking how very small and unvarying the Isle of Needles is and how limited its society. My father has a globe in his study, and on that our island is a mere pinprick. Yet it is all I have known. When I was a hoglet, I used to spend hours and hours looking at that globe, imagining myself in strange and exciting places - deserts, mountains, tropical forests and great cities... Oh, there is so much to see in the world, Mr Snipwicke, and I have seen so little of it! Indeed, until now, I have rather felt that life was passing me by."

"Oh dear, Miss Hoglinda!" said Snipwicke. "I fear you may be very disappointed by Gruntsey. It has neither deserts nor mountains, nor even tropical forests... and I must warn you that St Pricklier Port is merely a small town."

As he spoke, Spinet joined them. She laughed. "Take no notice of my brother, Miss Hoglinda! He likes to tease. I am convinced you will like Gruntsey very well indeed, for I can assure you it is quite charming."

"I do not deny it!" said Snipwicke. "But you must allow that it is also smaller than the Isle of Needles, its scenery is less varied and its society is... Well, its inhabitants are certainly fewer. I suspect Miss Hoglinda may not be so easily impressed as you, Spinet."

Hoglinda protested, "I am not so difficult to please as you would have me! Gruntsey will be different to the Isle of Needles, and that is enough for me." Then she smiled and added, "At least, it will be enough for now."

The three hedgehogs laughed and then continued to chat for a while. Gradually they got to know each other a little better. Until this moment, relations between Snipwicke and Hoglinda had been merely business-like. She had put her trust in him because she had to trust someone; but she had not forgotten that he was a smuggler - not just a dabbler like herself but a confirmed criminal of many years, whose dishonest trade depended upon lies and deception. Now, however, as the three hedgehogs chatted, she began to see another side to him, for Spinet revealed more about her brother than he was ever likely to have revealed himself.

Snipwicke and Spinet were evidently very close, and Hoglinda could understand why. Like her, they had lost their mother when they were young hoglets and had often been left alone at home while their father went to sea. Of course, in Admiral Hoglander's case, it was the navy that called him away, while Snipwicke's and Spinet's father was out smuggling contraband. And, while Hoglinda had been watched over by her governess, Snipwicke and Spinet had been left to do much as they pleased. Their days were spent climbing trees, roaming the countryside and, in the summer months, even bathing in the sea. As Snipwicke grew older, he began to join his father on his smuggling runs, and even Spinet was allowed to come along from time to time. Hoglinda thought it sounded idyllic. Then, however, their father had died, leaving them orphaned and almost penniless. From that time, Snipwicke devoted himself to looking after Spinet and would have continued to do so, had she not insisted on making her own way in the world, as soon as she was old enough.

The most surprising thing Hoglinda learned about Snipwicke, however, was that he was capable of great honesty, despite his dishonest trade. A couple of years back, the Preventives had seized some brandy belonging to him. When he discovered where they were keeping it, he broke into their storeroom to find it piled high with contraband - not only his own but everything they had confiscated from other smugglers over the previous month or so. It was more than he could have brought over by himself in the course of an entire year - and probably worth well over a thousand pounds. Another smuggler would probably have helped himself to a little extra; but Snipwicke took only what was rightfully his.

As the three hedgehogs chatted, Hoglinda found herself warming to both Snipwicke and Spinet. With such pleasant company to distract her, she hardly noticed the biting wind or the roughness of the crossing. And, when they were not chatting, there was still plenty to interest her. She watched closely as Snipwicke, Rip and Tar went about their business - counting knots, checking the compass and chart, adjusting the sails...

In the early afternoon, they all sat down for a meal of bread and cheese, washed down with beer. At half past four, they watched the sun slip below the horizon. Then, at around ten o'clock, those who could settled down for the night. A couple of mattresses were rolled out for Hoglinda and Spinet, while Snipwicke, Rip and Tar took it in

turns to rest and then only had the bare boards to sleep upon. Despite the relative luxury of her mattress, Hoglinda slept very little that night, being used as she was to sleeping in a warm bed. Yet, much as she liked her creature comforts, she had no regrets. After a lifetime of being left behind, she was at last going on a voyage of her own.

Chapter Ten
14th - 15th January 1778

It was a little before eleven o'clock the next morning when Gruntsey came into view. They had finally arrived, after twenty-two hours at sea. Hoglinda took out her spyglass and examined the low, rocky coastline. Here and there were white sandy beaches where the sea faded to turquoise, contrasting with the wintry blue of the sky above. She smiled. Gruntsey promised to be everything she had hoped for: as beautiful as the Isle of Needles but different and exciting.

As they rounded a corner and sailed down Gruntsey's east coast, the land began to rise a little. Then Belle Gratte Bay came into view, with St Pricklier Port at its southern end. Lining the waterfront and climbing up into the hillside behind were numerous handsome stone houses – more solid-looking and taller than anything Hoglinda had seen before – some as much as four or even five storeys high. In the centre of the port was the harbour. This was packed with vessels of every size and from every corner of the globe. Hoglinda thought it seemed even busier than her own island's capital, Nippert.

When they had disembarked, Snipwicke took rooms for them at the *Auberge d'Epine*, where they had a good view of the whole seafront.

Their plan was this. Hoglinda was to watch for the arrival of the *Hogspur*, with Snipwicke, Rip and Tar taking the occasional turn so she could stretch her legs – for they knew the *Hogspur* as well as she did; but she would be the chief look-out, and Spinet would keep her company. This left Snipwicke and his crew free to get on with their other business – buying provisions for the return journey and, of course, some brandy, tea and lace to smuggle back into the Isle of Needles. Snipwicke would also use his meetings with the Gruntsey merchants to pick up what information he could about Espinon, his activities and any contacts he might be known to have in Gruntsey. But, as soon as the *Hogspur* was spotted in the bay, they would all drop what they were doing. Hoglinda would remain in her room and become sole look-out, since she was the only one who actually knew what Espinon looked like and, furthermore, could not risk being seen herself. Meanwhile, Snipwicke, Rip and Tar would position themselves on the waterfront, waiting for Espinon to disembark and ready to follow him at Hoglinda's signal. Spinet would act as a messenger between Hoglinda and the others.

As soon as they had settled into their rooms, Hoglinda placed a chair in front of her window and began to survey the scene below, with her spyglass to the ready. The quayside was bristling with hedgehogs arriving and leaving, supervising the transfer of their cargo or arguing over prices. On the south pier, an auction was taking place. Along the esplanade, well-dressed hedgehogs strolled up and down in a leisurely fashion, stopping every now and then to chat with their friends. But there was no sign yet of Monsieur Espinon or the *Hogspur*.

The *Rapière* should still be in port, thought Hoglinda; this was the ship which had brought Espinon from Furze to Gruntsey and which he hoped would now take him back again. Hoglinda could see several ships flying Furzish colours, but their names were impossible to make out, even with the aid of her spyglass. She turned to Spinet for assistance. She had been pacing about the room at a loose end for quite a while now.

Pleased to be given something to do, Spinet dashed downstairs. Passing the public room, she glanced through the open doorway and noticed her brother ensconced at one of the tables. Snipwicke had, in fact, been on his way out to visit a wine merchant but had then bumped into a couple of old acquaintances: Le Sieur Erisse, a local cooper, and Mr Tippett, a smuggler from Pinzance in Great Bristlin. When they invited him to join them at their table, it seemed a good opportunity to pick up any news.

97

"Well now, Mr Snipwicke," said Erisse. "I didn't expect to see you back in Gruntsey quite so soon. Is business picking up a little now?"

"Yes, in a way," said Snipwicke, trying to be truthful. Though his smuggling business was not improving, Hoglinda had paid him well for this trip. Indeed, her generosity had made him a little uncomfortable, and he had briefly considered refusing to accept the full sum.

"So Mr Quiller no longer undercuts you then?" said Tippett, who naturally knew nothing of Hoglinda. "I am very glad to hear it."

"Oh, he does his best," responded Snipwicke, "but I have a new investor now and hope to get the better of Quiller after all."

"Something similar happened to me a while back," mused Tippett. "At first I thought it would send me under. Fortunately, I had the support of the community, which my competitor did not."

"I seem to remember," said Erisse, "that your competitor left the country in the end. Is that right?"

Tippett nodded. "Yes, I heard he went to live in the colonies."

"But it's very unlikely that *Quiller* will ever leave the country," said Snipwicke, who was determined not to let the conversation drift. "He's popular, rich and well connected across almost the whole of the Isle of Needles. Alas, my own influence does not extend so far. I have tried appealing to his better nature, of course, but he does not reply to my letters. And, when I attempted to call upon him last week," he added – lying now, in the hope of learning more, "well, his housekeeper told me he was away. I am not entirely sure I believed her..."

"When exactly was this – that you called upon him?" asked Erisse.

"Oh, last Thursday. Why do you ask?"

"Because the housekeeper spoke the truth, Mr Snipwicke. Mr Quiller was here then, in St Pricklier Port. Monsieur Grattage, the harbour master, happened to mention it to me."

"Oh, I see!" said Snipwicke, who had got just the response he wanted. "I wonder what brought him to Gruntsey. He usually leaves that side of the business to Mr Cutliss."

"True, but he does come here from time to time," said Erisse. "I understand that on this occasion he met a hedgehog by the name of Espinon. Apparently, he's a wine grower from Pawdeaux and is hoping to export his wines to Gruntsey. In fact, I know several merchants here who have received letters from him, requesting a meeting. But I cannot think what his business with Quiller might be – unless Quiller now intends to sail all the way to Pawdeaux for his wine."

"He is a fool if he does," cut in Tippett.

"And we all know that Quiller is no fool," said Snipwicke. Then he added, as casually as he could: "Perhaps, therefore, it was something else that he wished to discuss with Monsieur Espinon..."

Neither Erisse nor Tippett responded to this comment. But Snipwicke was unwilling to let the subject go.

"How did you happen to hear about Monsieur Espinon?" he asked.

"From Monsieur Grattage," said Erisse, yawning a little, for he began to find their present conversation rather dull. "Mr Snipwicke, if this matter interests you so very much, I suggest you ask Monsieur Espinon yourself – I believe he is still in port. Certainly his ship is not yet sailed. *Rapière* is her name. Why don't you enquire after him there?"

Snipwicke shrugged to indicate that his interest was nothing more than curiosity. Then, catching sight of his sister in the passage beyond – for she had just darted back in from the street – he excused himself and hurried after her.

"Spinet!" he whispered, as he caught her up on the stairs. "What have you learnt?"

"Only that the *Rapière* is still here and shows no sign of making sail. And you?"

Snipwicke repeated his conversation with Le Sieur Erisse and Mr Tippett.

"Are you acquainted with Monsieur Grattage?" asked Spinet.

"Yes, he's the harbour master. He knows every ship in St Pricklier Port and generally makes everybody else's business his own. So there is a good chance he may have picked up some further information about Espinon. I think I should call on him – I can easily find some excuse or other, and now is as good a time as any."

So saying, he turned tail, leaving Spinet to pass on the news to Hoglinda.

"Is it far to the harbour master's office?" asked Hoglinda, when Spinet had finished her explanations.

"No, it's in Thornton Street, which is just off the southern end of the esplanade." Spinet drew up a chair next to Hoglinda, whose spyglass was just then pointed at the *Rapière*. "Can you see much sign of activity on board?" she asked.

"They appear to be mending one of the sails," said Hoglinda. "So I think she'll stay put for a while yet. Certainly Monsieur Espinon was not expecting her to sail before tomorrow, at the earliest."

"Of course, yes – I had forgotten that," said Spinet. Then she added, "When I was down on the quayside just now, I could see neither Rip nor Tar. Can you see either of them now?"

"No... Yes, they are walking back towards the *Sea Urchin.*"

"I wonder if I should go down," said Spinet, "and show them where the *Rapière* is."

"Oh, I should think they will have found that out for themselves by now, don't you?"

"Yes, I suppose they must have." Spinet stayed where she was but was clearly restless and, with nothing better to do, began to hum a tune.

"That's pretty," said Hoglinda. "What is it?"

"It's a piece by Clawrelli. I've been teaching it to Flora and Fauna – the two hoglets in my charge. They are both learning to play the spinet."

"How delightful! Why, I think I envy you a little. I would love to teach my niece and nephew to play; but, alas, there is no instrument in Quiller's house."

"Do not envy me, Miss Hoglinda! I am very fond of Flora and Fauna; but the life of a governess is a lonely one, for I am neither a servant nor one of the family."

100

Hoglinda stopped looking through her spyglass and reflected for a moment. She had been educated by a governess herself; and, though very fond of her, she had always been conscious of the social difference between them. What had never occurred to her until now was how her governess might feel about her situation – never truly belonging to one group or another. Hoglinda felt a wave of shame.

"You are quite right," she said at last. "Please forgive me for speaking so thoughtlessly. At least, I hope, there need be no such difficulties between *us*. Indeed, though we have only known each other such a short time, I feel we are already become friends."

"Why, yes, Miss Hoglinda, I feel that, too," said Spinet, smiling brightly.

"Well then, we may do without the 'Miss' - may we not, Spinet?"

"Yes, Hoglinda, I think we may!"

The two hedgehogs smiled happily at one another. Then Hoglinda turned back to look out of the window once more, while Spinet returned to humming her tune. Not long afterwards, Snipwicke came back from the harbour master's office, but he had no further news to report. Monsieur Grattage was away and not expected back until the following day. Snipwicke's enquiries about Espinon would have to wait.

The rest of the day passed uneventfully. Snipwicke finished ordering his cargo for the return journey, Rip and Tar were busy on the boat, and Spinet called on an old friend. Hoglinda, however, spent most of the time alone in her room, gazing out of the window and feeling increasingly restless.

The following morning began in a similar fashion. Hoglinda remained stuck in her room. And, though at least she had Spinet for company once again, the time seemed to pass more slowly than ever. Staring out of the window, checking her watch repeatedly, she began to wonder whether the *Hogspur* would ever appear. Then, just after ten o'clock, she had her answer: the *Hogspur* had arrived at last.

Spinet rushed out of the *auberge* to tell the others the news. She found Rip and Tar loading tea crates onto the *Sea Urchin*; but Snipwicke had just gone off to call on the harbour master again, so they decided to manage without him.

The *Hogspur* docked just inside the harbour walls. Hoglinda watched as a group of hedgehogs disembarked into the ship's boat and then rowed towards the quayside. There were four of them at the oars and two passengers, but they were too far away to identify. It was only when they came up the harbour steps, that Hoglinda could be quite certain; and now they were just feet away from Rip and Tar. The latter were chatting casually to each other, apparently taking no notice whatsoever of the *Hogspur's* arrival. Without moving his head, Rip glanced up at Hoglinda's window; and Hoglinda immediately grabbed the white shawl draped over the back of her chair.

"Is he there?" asked Spinet excitedly. "Which one is he?"

Hoglinda wrapped the white shawl around her shoulders. "Monsieur Espinon is the one in the dark grey jacket, with the red collar," she said, as she stood up next to the window to make sure she could be seen by Rip and Tar: her white shawl was the agreed signal.

"The hedgehog he's talking to," she continued, "that's Mr Cutliss… Oh and there's Pinaft - carrying Monsieur Espinon's bag for him, I believe!"

Spinet leapt to her feet. "I'll tell the others at once," she said and dashed out.

But Rip had already noted Hoglinda's signal. He passed word to Tar, who was facing the little group from the *Hogspur*. Tar was acquainted with Cutliss and the crew, so he was able to single out Espinon without difficulty. He watched him out of the corner of his eye. He and Cutliss were discussing something. But a moment later they shook paws, and Espinon set off towards the north esplanade - followed by Pinaft with his bag. Spinet arrived on the scene at almost the same moment. But, seeing Tar set off in pursuit, she made no attempt to pass on her message. Instead, she hung back in the shadows, watching as first Espinon and Pinaft, and then Tar, disappeared into the crowd.

Tar had no trouble keeping up with Espinon, for he walked slowly, looking to left and right as he went, apparently searching for someone. He had not gone far when he was approached by a Furzish naval officer. The two of them exchanged a few words and the officer pointed to a Furzish naval frigate: it was the *Rapière*. Then they parted company. Pinaft - and Espinon's bag - remained with the Furzish

officer; but Espinon himself went back along the esplanade the way he had come.

Tar waited for him to pass and then turned round himself. Espinon had quickened his pace now, forcing Tar to do the same and to narrow the gap between them. Then, just as they were approaching the harbour again, Mr Cutliss looked up. Their eyes met. Tar touched his hat by way of a greeting, and Cutliss nodded back - his manner friendly enough. But Tar was worried. It was surely impossible to keep on following Espinon now, without arousing suspicion. He rejoined Rip, who had not moved from his spot.

"Has summat happened?" asked Rip.

"I been noticed by Mr Cutliss, that's what's happened," said Tar. "Trouble es, we don't want to let the skipper down, but I reckons as t'wudden't be no safer if *thee* followed aater en, neither."

Rip smiled. "Don't look now, mayet, but Miss Spinet be jest over thirt. Her'll do better than either of we, for Mr Cutliss don't know she."

Spinet was, indeed, still lurking in the shadows and had seen what had happened. She waited for Espinon to pass. Then she stepped out into the sunlight and followed after him, just as Rip had hoped. Unable to see his face, she focussed instead on his dark grey jacket and its distinctive red collar. She followed him down to the far end of the esplanade and then away from the seafront. The street here was narrow and so busy with hedgehogs going about their business that Spinet began to worry she might lose Espinon in the crowd.

"Well, I never! If isn't Mademoiselle Spinet!" said a voice from the other side of the street.

The speaker had a Gruntsey accent and his voice sounded familiar, but this was no time for renewing old acquaintances. Pretending not to have heard, Spinet pressed on; but, a moment later, the other hedgehog was standing right in front of her, blocking her way.

"Mademoiselle Spinet!" he said again, beaming. "What a wonderful surprise! But what brings you to Gruntsey? Are you come with your brother?"

"Oh, Monsieur Renifleur!" she exclaimed; for she did, indeed, recognize him, now that he was in front of her. He had been a friend of her father's, and she had dined at his house on her past visits to Gruntsey. "How lovely it is to see you! But I am afraid you must excuse me, for I am in something of a hurry." As she glanced over his shoulder, she could see Espinon disappearing down the street.

"Oh, I am sure whatever it is can wait. What occasion can you have to be in such a hurry? Now, let me persuade you - and your brother, for I presume he is here? - let me persuade you both to dine with my wife and me tonight."

"Forgive me," insisted Spinet, "I really must - "

She stopped mid-sentence; for, when she looked over Renifleur's shoulder this time, Espinon was nowhere to be seen. There were several roads leading off this one, and it was impossible to tell which way he had gone. Yet she was determined not to give up. Making her excuses, she declined the invitation as politely as she could. Then she hurried on, taking the very first turning she came to. But it was no good: she had lost him. Crestfallen, she turned back towards the quayside to look for Rip and Tar.

* * *

Back in the *Auberge d'Epine*, Hoglinda drummed her claws on the arm of her chair, wondering what to do next. She was under strict instructions not to show her face while Espinon was around; but he had left the harbour front now. As for Cutliss and his crew, she had just seen them disappear into a neighbouring *auberge*, no doubt seeking refreshment; she imagined they would be some time. So the coast was clear now, and it occurred to her that Snipwicke really ought to be told the news. Grabbing her jacket, hat and gloves, she hurried out of the *auberge* in the direction of the harbour master's office.

* * *

Earlier that morning, when Snipwicke had arrived at the harbour master's office, he had found Monsieur Grattage already busy with someone else. He decided to wait. Eleven o'clock came and went. So he got up from his seat and began to examine the pictures on the walls. Several were of St Pricklier Port, naturally. Another one, he thought, was probably neighbouring St Nailier...

"*Monsieur*," said a voice behind him. Snipwicke turned. It was no one he knew - just another visitor for Monsieur Grattage. The newcomer made a little bow towards Snipwicke, which Snipwicke returned. Then they both sat down.

With nothing better to do, Snipwicke examined the stranger out of the corner of his eye. He was of average height, slim and elegant. His clothes were smart but not showy; the only touch of colour was the red collar on his dark grey jacket. Beyond his polite greeting, however, he seemed disinclined to chat. So Snipwicke forgot about the stranger, and his thoughts turned instead to Hoglinda and the others. Had Espinon arrived yet, he wondered? And, if so, had they been able to identify his contact?

"Bonjour, messieurs," said a female voice. A pretty hedgehog in a green coat had just walked into the room, with a vase of dried flowers in one paw and her hat and gloves in the other. Snipwicke supposed she must be Madame Hérispionne, the wife of Monsieur Grattage. The two visitors rose from their chairs, but she motioned to them to keep their seats. Placing the vase on a small table, she stepped back to consider the arrangement. Then, apparently satisfied, she put on her hat and gloves and left.

Snipwicke looked at his watch. It was now ten minutes past eleven o'clock: he had been waiting almost an hour. He wondered whether he should give up on Monsieur Grattage and go back to the others. Clearly he was not the only one feeling impatient: for shortly afterwards, the other visitor got up and left, though he had waited barely five minutes.

Hoglinda was just a few yards away from the harbour master's office when, to her astonishment, she saw Espinon emerge from within. He paused at the bottom of the steps for a moment, looking to left and right as though searching for someone. Hoglinda hastily pulled her hat down over her eyes and, when he turned and began to walk in the opposite direction, she breathed a sigh of relief. But what should she do now? There was no sign of Rip or Tar. Perhaps they had already witnessed Espinon's meeting and were on their way back. But what if they had not? It suddenly occurred to her that Espinon and Snipwicke might have met in the harbour master's office, without either of them having the slightest idea who the other was. She was tempted to go in and tell Snipwicke; but instinct told her to follow Espinon instead. The place was bristling with hedgehogs and, as long as she was careful, it seemed unlikely she would be spotted.

So she followed Espinon down the street, weaving her way through the crowds as she went. Every now and then, she would lose sight of him but then find him again a moment later. Eventually the crowds began to thin out. It was at this point that she realized he was no longer alone. His companion, moreover, was female. Hoglinda felt sure this must be the meeting they had all been expecting and that *she* must be the hedgehog Quiller was to report to - 'Madame X', as Snipwicke had put it. She tried to commit her description to memory - a little below

107

average height, a black hat, a long green coat. Her face, however, was unfortunately hidden from view.

It was not long before they had left St Pricklier Port behind. The road climbed steeply now, winding its way up between tree-clad hills, with just the occasional house set back from the street. Then quite suddenly, it seemed, the crowds disappeared. There was just Espinon, his companion, one other hedgehog walking in the opposite direction, and herself. Hoglinda felt horribly exposed. While she was still deciding whether to carry on or not, Espinon and his companion suddenly turned back. Hoglinda was horrified. In a few moments, they would pass each other. Her legs felt so weak she feared she would keel over, but she *had* to carry on. Keeping her head down and her eyes fixed on the road, she passed them and they fell silent. Had Espinon recognized her? Surely not. The upper part of her face was well hidden, thanks to her large-brimmed hat. And, if he *had* recognized her, would he really have just let her pass? Their silence did, however, confirm her suspicions that this was no casual meeting: Espinon's companion was indeed 'Madame X'.

Hoglinda was now more determined than ever not to lose them. As soon as their footsteps had receded into the distance, she turned round. They were out of sight now. But, more afraid than ever of being spotted, she paused at the next corner and peered ahead. They had stopped and were deep in conversation but too far away for her to hear them. Fortunately, there was a gate in one of the walls running along either side of the road. Hoglinda slipped through the gate and found herself in a cottage garden. The cottage shutters were closed and there appeared to be no one about. So, crouching down, she followed the wall until she was roughly level with Espinon and his contact. She knelt down on the damp grass and listened. They were speaking in Furzish - quietly but clearly.

"So you see," said Espinon, "we cannot proceed at present - not until we have identified this Bristlish spy. That is why I must now return to Furze."

"So it was all for nothing!" said his companion.

"Not necessarily. Once the matter of the Bristlish spy has been attended to, I believe the invasion may still go ahead - perhaps even in November as we planned."

"But surely that is impossible!" responded his companion. "The Bristlish are bound to reinforce the Isle of Needles' defences, now they know of your plan. Why, by November, they may even have built

some additional forts. The invasion - if there is still to be one - must be moved to the mainland."

"No, Hérispionne, I cannot agree. Moving the invasion would mean starting from scratch, and that would very probably delay us by another year. What is more, it is far too good a plan to be cast aside - the Isle of Needles is too perfect a spot. And we do not know for certain that its defences will be much strengthened. The Bristlish forces are already very stretched, and they will soon be fighting on both sides of the ocean. I doubt they will want to concentrate their forces on the Isle of Needles, if that means leaving their mainland unguarded. As for building more forts, they have little money to spare for it. You know how desperate their government is for money - how they keep on increasing their taxes and thinking up new ones time and again. And to so little effect, thanks to our smuggling friends!"

Hoglinda was shocked to hear him voice an opinion which had once been her own. But, though she now felt a prick of conscience, this was no time for introspection.

"Well, perhaps you are right," conceded Hérispionne. "Indeed, I *hope* you are, but you cannot make any assumptions… Perhaps you should ask Mr Quiller to keep you informed. He could report to you on the state of the island's defences, could he not?"

"He could - and indeed he shall, for I have already engaged him to do just that. He was a little reluctant at first. Having originally expected us to meet with no resistance, he has now begun to worry that there may be casualties among the islanders. He still regards them as his friends, you see - which I can understand, of course - though whether they would feel the same way about him, if they knew the truth, I doubt very much."

"It is a little late in the day to have such scruples," said Hérispionne impatiently. "But thank goodness he does not know of our plan to expel the island's inhabitants after we've taken over."

"Thank goodness indeed, for I believe that *would* turn him against us. Especially as he will have to leave the island himself, if he wishes to keep his association with us a secret. Happily, there is little danger of him finding out... That is, unless *you* tell him!"

Espinon chuckled. But Hérispionne did not appear to understand the joke.

"I!" she exclaimed. "I have never even met him!"

"No, but you shall, for I told him to report to you. That way he need commit nothing to paper. But don't worry, I have told him nothing about you - neither your name nor that you're the harbour master's wife. He knows only that he must come to Gruntsey whenever he has anything to report, and that *you* will find *him*."

"I see. Well, I shall have to take care that I don't come across him in my husband's office, but that should not be too difficult."

"Thank you, Hérispionne. I knew I could count upon you."

"You know I am always happy to serve my country, Espinon. But, talking of my husband, I really must be getting back now, for I promised I would help him with his book-keeping. Unless there is anything else you wish to discuss?"

"Nothing. Indeed, I must be going myself, for my ship is ready to sail. They are only waiting for me to come aboard."

With that, Espinon and Hérispionne walked on. Hoglinda listened to their retreating footsteps; but it was a full half hour before she finally dared emerge from her hiding place and set off back to the *auberge*. As she entered the building, she met Snipwicke coming down the stairs.

"Miss Hoglinda!" he exclaimed. "Wherever have you been? You have had us all worried. I've been up and down the harbour a dozen times looking for you - and was just now on my way to seek help."

"Oh, I am so sorry, Mr Snipwicke. I only went out to find you to tell you of Espinon's arrival. But, when I reached the harbour master's office, I - "

"Ah, yes, the harbour master's office," said Snipwicke grimly, before she could finish. "That was another wasted visit - in more ways than one." He then related how he had finally given up on Monsieur Grattage and returned to find Spinet in a terrible state, after losing Espinon in the crowd. "What is more," he said, "when Spinet described Espinon to me, I realized that I, too, had had him within my grasp. Can you believe it? He was there in the waiting room with me, at the harbour master's office! And all for nothing! I fear now that Espinon's meeting with the mysterious Madame X has most likely already taken place, in which case we can have little hope of identifying her."

"Oh, the meeting has certainly taken place, Mr Snipwicke," said Hoglinda.

"Whatever do you mean?"

"I was there."

The expression on Snipwicke's face was everything Hoglinda had hoped for by way of astonishment, delight and admiration. However, she waited until they had rejoined Spinet upstairs before relaying her news in full. When she told them of the Furzish plan to expel the entire population of the Isle of Needles, the mood quickly changed. Spinet was shocked and speechless. Snipwicke was angry.

"This is too much!" he exclaimed, bristling with anger. "Quiller may be your cousin, Miss Hoglinda, but there are limits to my - "

"You misunderstand me," interrupted Hoglinda. "Quiller has no idea that this was part of the plan. Espinon was convinced Quiller would turn against them if he should find out. He has not forgotten how Quiller hesitated when he was asked to report on the Isle of Needles' defences."

"Hesitated!" scoffed Snipwicke. "That was very fine of him, I am sure!" Then he added sharply, "He still agreed to do it, did he not?"

"Never mind that now," said Spinet, with animation. "We can use this new information. We can turn Mr Quiller against them! More than that, if we can get Mr Quiller on our side, he could feed Madame Hérispionne with false information - he could convince the Furzish to abandon their plans!"

Hoglinda and Snipwicke stared at Spinet. She had hit the nail on the head, and they both knew it. For the first time in days, Hoglinda felt truly happy; for she no longer feared that Snipwicke would hand Quiller over to the law. At last, there was a way out for her cousin; and she felt sure he must take it.

That evening, the *Rapière* set sail for Furze, with Espinon on board. Hoglinda spotted him on deck as she sat looking through her spyglass. But, as there seemed to be no reason to rush back to the Isle of Needles - for there was no immediate threat, Hoglinda and Snipwicke agreed to allow themselves one more day in Gruntsey. Hoglinda fully intended to spend that time enjoying herself, finally exploring the island properly; and Spinet was more than happy to keep her company. The *Hogspur* also remained in port; but Mr Cutliss and his crew never seemed to wander much beyond the seafront, so Hoglinda decided she could explore the rest of the island without fear of discovery.

The following morning, Snipwicke joined Hoglinda and his sister for a walk, up the hill behind St Pricklier Port, where they had a good view of the entire bay. But then he returned once more to the harbour master's office. This time he succeeded in seeing Monsieur Grattage. He made no mention of Espinon, as he had originally planned to do. Instead he concentrated on finding out what he could about his wife, Madame Hérispionne. It was not a subject which could be introduced easily in the course of such a meeting. But, when the business was done, Snipwicke took the opportunity to ask after his wife's health.

"Oh, she is very well, thank you. Indeed, Hérispionne is so active that she quite puts me to shame. She not only runs the household but helps me run the office, too. Really, she can put her paw to anything she chooses! I cannot imagine what I would do without her."

"Indeed!" said Snipwicke. "Well, you are very lucky to have such a wife... As it happens, I believe I may have seen her when I called yesterday - but I may be mistaken, for I have not yet had the pleasure of being introduced to her."

"Well, no, we have not been married long. In fact, Hérispionne is not from Gruntsey at all. She is Furzish, from a Hoguenot family - one of the few families not driven into exile during the Furzish Wars of Religion. Thankfully, life is much easier for her here than it was in her own country. There she and her family were forced to live very quietly. They mixed little with their neighbours."

"How did you meet her?"

"Oh, her uncle is a wine dealer - in Pawdeaux. He seldom comes to Gruntsey in person but, happily for me, he did come last summer and brought his niece with him. It was love at first sight!"

"How wonderful!" said Snipwicke, as though he really meant it.

At this point, Snipwicke decided to take his leave of Grattage. He had heard enough now to be convinced that he was no traitor but an innocent victim in all of this. For, while it might have been love at first sight for Grattage, Snipwicke suspected this had not been the case for Hérispionne. He rather doubted she was from a persecuted Hoguenot family at all. It was far more likely that she had made up the story to pave the way for her marriage to the harbour master - the one hedgehog who knew all the comings and goings in St Pricklier Port. And it was little wonder she made herself so useful to him, helping him to run his office. That way, everything he knew, she knew too.

Snipwicke made his way back to the *Auberge d'Epine*, where he had arranged to meet Hoglinda and Spinet. He arrived shortly after noon, and they were just sitting down to luncheon. Though it was not a meal he was accustomed to take, they persuaded him to join them; but he had barely sat down one minute, when there was a disturbance outside which drew him to the window.

"What's happening?" asked Spinet.

"It looks as though a fight has broken out," said Snipwicke.

Hoglinda got up and took a closer look with the aid of her spyglass. Just beyond the crowd - and clearly the focus of the commotion - were three hedgehogs dressed in uniform.

"How very odd!" she said, "The Bristlish Navy are there - I can see three officers and about a dozen sailors armed with clubs. They seem to be involved in some sort of confrontation with the crowd. Every time the crowd threatens to get too close, the sailors raise their clubs. Take a look for yourself, Mr Snipwicke."

Snipwicke looked through Hoglinda's spyglass. The navy group were moving on now, and he followed them along the harbour front. Then suddenly Cutliss came into view. Pushing his way to the front of the crowd, Cutliss approached one of the officers and pointed to the *Sea Urchin*. The officer nodded. Then, taking four sailors with him, he boarded the *Sea Urchin*, and there accosted Rip and Tar. There followed what looked like an argument, which ended swiftly with the sailors grabbing Rip and Tar and dragging them down the gangplank.

Snipwicke was horrified. He immediately dashed downstairs and out into the street, only to find his way blocked by the crowds. By the time he reached the front, Rip and Tar were nowhere to be seen; but Cutliss was still there. Snipwicke slunk back into the crowd and, assuming a casual tone, asked the hedgehog next to him what the commotion was all about.

" 'Tis the press gang," said his neighbour, contemptuously. The press gang was part of the Bristlish Navy, with powers to recruit into

its ranks any seafaring hedgehogs it chose - by force and without warning.

"But surely they can have no authority here in Gruntsey?" said Snipwicke in disbelief.

"Not over us Gruntsey islanders," said the other hedgehog, "but they are rounding up all the Bristlish sailors they can lay their paws on. If I were you, I'd get out of here pretty sharpish."

Though, deep down, Snipwicke knew it was a hopeless case, he wracked his brains for *something* he could do to help his friends. While he hesitated, Cutliss saw him. For a second their eyes met, and Cutliss smiled malevolently. Then he rushed over to the navy officer he had spoken to before and pointed in Snipwicke's direction.

Snipwicke did not wait to see how the officer would respond but turned tail and fled. Forcing his way through the crowd, he ignored the protests of the hedgehogs he had to push aside, every now and then glancing over his shoulder, looking for his pursuers. But he was too

fast for them. By the time he reached the *auberge,* he knew he was safe. He rejoined the others and relayed to them the unhappy news.

Spinet was distraught. Like her brother, she had known Rip and Tar all her life. Hoglinda was also deeply troubled - all the more so because her father was an admiral of the Bristlish Navy. What was *his* opinion of the press gang, she wondered? Great Bristlin prided itself

116

on the freedom of its subjects. But this was not freedom! Still, it was foolish to worry about the rights and wrongs of it now, when there were other more pressing questions to be answered.

"Mr Snipwicke," she said. "Why do you think Mr Cutliss betrayed you? I thought there was a code of honour between free traders! And why did the press gang take Rip and Tar but not Mr Cutliss and his crew?"

"I can only imagine that Cutliss bought his freedom - and that of his crew. No doubt the crew of the *Sea Urchin* was a part of the price... I'm afraid this unhappy event leaves us high and dry, for it may take me several days to find a new crew."

"A new crew!" exclaimed Spinet. "Snipwicke, you are surely not intending to abandon Rip and Tar!"

"I am sorry, Spinet, but there is really nothing I can do to help them. I am as upset as you are, and I would help them if I could - but I can't. We must face facts."

"But surely..." began Spinet. Then she turned to Hoglinda, "Hoglinda, could *you* not speak to the naval lieutenant on their behalf? Once he knows you are Admiral Hoglander's daughter, he will surely listen."

"Out of the question," said Snipwicke, before Hoglinda was able to reply. "It would look very ill for Miss Hoglinda to be taking such a keen interest in a couple of suspected smugglers!"

Spinet looked downcast. "Yes, I suppose it would... I'm sorry, Hoglinda... But, Snipwicke, you must at least promise me that you will be careful yourself. Please lie low for a while, until the press gang are gone."

"If it will save you from worrying. But it will add a further delay, for I cannot lie low and find a crew at the same time; and, while there is no absolute necessity for us to hurry back, I confess I shall not be easy until we have spoken to Quiller. What say you, Miss Hoglinda?"

"I agree with Spinet - that is, I agree you should lie low for now - especially as the press gang may not be our only problem. You see, Mr Snipwicke, I was watching Mr Cutliss when he pointed you out to the lieutenant. I saw the way he smiled - the pleasure he took in betraying you."

"Well, that is perhaps understandable, for he is devoted to Quiller."

"But *you* have done Mr Quiller no injury!" protested Spinet. "It is the other way round!"

117

"True, but we have quarrelled and it would be natural for Cutliss to dislike me. But don't worry - once the press gang are gone, he will pay me no further attention."

"Unless he wants you out of the way," suggested Hoglinda.

"What do you mean?" asked Snipwicke.

"Well, what if it was more than mere dislike that moved him to betray you? What if he suspects your true purpose in coming here?"

"But why should he suspect? Even assuming that Quiller has told Cutliss everything - that he knows about Espinon's meeting with Madame Hérispionne, there is nothing to connect *my* presence with any of this. After all, it is perfectly natural for me to visit Gruntsey - and Cutliss knows that."

"True..." agreed Hoglinda. She pondered for a moment and then an unpleasant thought occurred to her. "Perhaps Mr Cutliss saw me with you this morning, when we were out walking. Oh, if only I had stayed inside! I thought it would be safe away from the harbour with Monsieur Espinon now gone. But - if Mr Cutliss *has* seen me - he will know I have lied to Quiller and must surely suspect that I know what they are about. What more likely reason is there for my coming here so secretly with you - at precisely the same time as Monsieur Espinon?"

"Well, thank goodness Monsieur Espinon is gone then," said Spinet. "Mr Cutliss cannot warn him now."

Snipwicke frowned. "No, indeed, he cannot. But, if Miss Hoglinda is right and Cutliss does suspect we know of the plot, he must be very worried now. He will expect us to report our suspicions as soon as we are returned to the Isle of Needles - and would undoubtedly much prefer it if we never returned at all. Indeed, knowing the sort of hedgehog he is, I think he would very likely try to prevent our return."

"Prevent our return!" exclaimed Hoglinda. "But how? Surely you cannot mean..." Her voice tailed away. It was obvious what Snipwicke meant. She already knew Quiller's gang would resort to violence if necessary - and she could not assume that she and her friends would be spared simply because she was Quiller's cousin. "Well," she said, thoughtfully, "it seems to me there is only one course of action open to us. We must reason with him, as we plan to do with Quiller. Once he realizes the Furzish intend to expel the entire population of our island, he will surely want to have nothing more to do with Monsieur Espinon. I will speak to him myself."

"I doubt very much he will believe you," said Snipwicke. "He has the upper paw. He will just think you've made it up because you are afraid of him... No, after his betrayal of Rip and Tar, there can be no trust between us. When he betrayed them, he burnt his boats; and he knows it."

"So what do you propose we do?" asked Hoglinda.

"Well, the first thing is to find a new crew."

"But, Snipwicke, you already have another crew!" said Spinet. "You must remember that, when we sailed as hoglets, I knew the ropes as well as you. I am sure I can pick it up again quickly enough."

Snipwicke smiled indulgently. "Perhaps you will, Spinet, but it takes three hedgehogs to sail the *Sea Urchin*."

"We *are* three. You forget that Hoglinda is the daughter of an admiral."

"That is hardly a qualification - no offence, Miss Hoglinda."

"None taken, Mr Snipwicke. Though, as it happens, my father has taken me out in his yacht many times: I know how to hoist and reef a sail."

"I am impressed," said Snipwicke, truthfully. "And, if it were simply a matter of a pleasure outing in fine weather, I would be very happy to have the two of you as my crew. But crossing the Channel is a serious affair at the best of times - hedgehogs lose their lives at sea every year. No, for that, I need a strong and experienced crew."

"Ideally, yes," said Hoglinda. "But, if Mr Cutliss is as ruthless as you say he is, are we really safe even here? The longer we remain in St Pricklier Port, the greater the risk he will find us. Who knows what he may do then! And, when you do have your new crew - strong and experienced as they may be, Mr Snipwicke, that will not be enough to save us. Cutliss has only to follow us out to sea and then attack as soon as there is no one else around to witness it. You know as well as I do that we have no chance of outrunning the *Hogspur*. She is bigger and faster than the *Sea Urchin* - and, with her crew of fourteen, she will be certain to win paws down in any fight. No, we need to give ourselves a head start. It is surely our only hope. That means we have no time to find a new crew. I say we leave tonight, under cover of darkness."

"Under cover of darkness!" exclaimed Snipwicke. "That, I am afraid, is out of the question."

"But you are used to sailing in the dark, are you not?" said Spinet. "And surely it is easier to sail out of a harbour in the dark than to beach your boat on the Isle of Needles' dangerous shore?"

"On the contrary, Spinet. Have you not seen how crowded the harbour is? As for the Isle of Needles' coastline, that's an entirely different matter. It's my home. I know it like the back of my paw."

"So you plan to sail out under the *Hogspur's* nose in broad daylight, do you?" said Spinet. "After, of course, you have found your new crew."

Snipwicke hesitated. Hoglinda was right about giving themselves a head start. He looked out of the window: the sky was clear and the conditions were good. If they were lucky and the weather stayed like this for the whole voyage, then perhaps he could manage with just Spinet and Hoglinda for his crew, after all. But sailing out by night? He looked down at the harbour and, in his head, plotted a course from the quayside where the *Sea Urchin* was moored, threading his way between the other boats, past cutters, luggers, sloops and ketches, out towards the exit. Was that the answer? To work out the route in advance? To memorize the distances, the twists and the turns?

"Very well," he said at last, "I concede. We sail tonight - just the three of us and under cover of darkness."

The navy frigate sailed with the outgoing tide, taking with her the press gang and its unwilling recruits. By then the *Sea Urchin* and the *Hogspur* had been left high and dry; for they were both moored inside the harbour, which dried out as the sea retreated, leaving them resting on the mud. After nightfall, however, the tide would come in again and both the vessels would be afloat once more.

Hoglinda, Snipwicke and Spinet waited in Hoglinda's room, which not only overlooked the harbour but also had a good view of the entire bay. Taking out his map of Gruntsey, Snipwicke drew his chair up to the window and marked the location of every vessel currently moored there. Then he plotted his way out and memorized his plan. The remainder of the time he used to explain to Hoglinda and Spinet their tasks as his crew. Of course, it would have been a great deal easier if he could have shown them the ropes on board. But to board the *Sea Urchin* in daylight was out of the question with the *Hogspur* close by.

By the time this was all done, it was half past four in the afternoon. Just visible behind a thin veil of cloud, the faint smudge of the winter sun hung low in the sky. Snipwicke watched as the smudge slipped

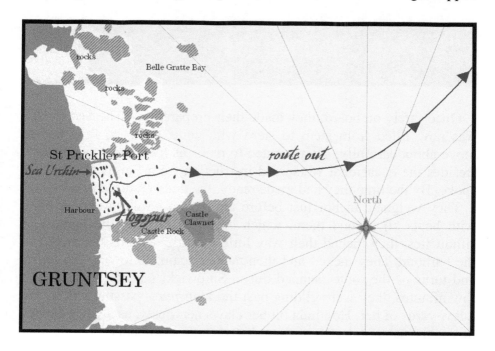

beneath the waves and the sky gradually darkened, until it was almost indistinguishable from the sea. And still he waited. At half past nine, just a little before high tide and with the *Sea Urchin* now afloat again, the three hedgehogs finally ventured out of the *auberge*. They walked in silence, their lanterns unlit - Snipwicke in front, the others keeping close behind. As they descended the slippery harbour steps, Spinet held on to her brother and Hoglinda held on to Spinet.

Once safely on board, they made their preparations. The *Sea Urchin* was now filled from stem to stern with contraband, so they had to move about carefully. They wanted to make as little noise as possible. Besides the occasional whispered instruction from Snipwicke, no one spoke. By the time they had made ready, the tide had turned.

They weighed anchor just before ten o'clock. Sailing almost blind with boats all around them, which appeared only as the faintest of silhouettes, they inched their way little by little towards the mouth of the harbour. They tacked and then tacked again, following the twists and turns of the route mapped out in Snipwicke's head. Then, after a few minutes, they were gliding past the *Hogspur* - passing within just a few yards of her. Hoglinda bit her claws nervously, as a voice floated across the narrow stretch of water between the two boats.

"So, Mr Cutliss, how long do you reckon it'll take 'en to find a new crew?"

"Oh, I don't rightly know. A few days, I suppose. 'Tis a great shame the press gang didn't get him. That way we'd only have Miss Hoglinda to deal with - oh, and that other hedgehog I saw 'em with, whoever she may be. No, we could have got rid of *them two* easy enough, but with Snipwicke still around, it'll be a great deal harder. We may even have to let 'em sail and then deal with 'em at sea."

"Oh, I wudden't mind that," said the other hedgehog. "A little sea fighting always lifts my spirits."

Cutliss chuckled; but then the voices faded into the distance. On board the *Sea Urchin,* they had heard every word and now knew Hoglinda's fears to be justified. But no one spoke. The *Sea Urchin* slipped out of St Pricklier Port unheard and unseen.

Once they were a safe distance from the harbour, they lit and hoisted a lantern. Then they eased out the mainsail and bore north-east. This put the wind behind them; but they took it slow and steady, and kept the mainsail reefed, for they were not yet in the open sea. Ahead lay a narrow passage, between Gruntsey and a smaller island, where there were dangerous rocks and ledges. A single miscalculation or clumsy manoeuvre, and they could be wrecked. Hoglinda and Spinet

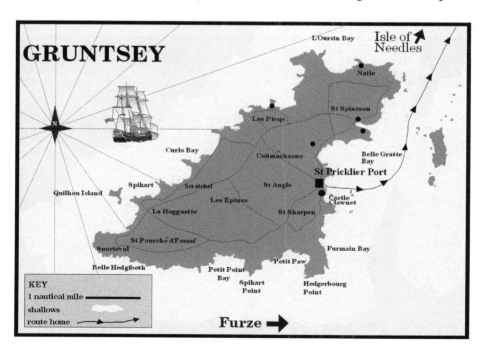

ran out the log-line, while Snipwicke watched the sandglass, to calculate their speed. Then Snipwicke checked his compass and noted their position on his chart. The three of them then repeated this exercise again, every few minutes for almost an hour, until at last they were clear.

Now nothing lay between them and home. Breathing a sigh of relief, they shook out the reefs in the mainsail to bring it to full size, so as to catch as much wind as possible. They then decided to get some rest, taking turns to do so. Hoglinda went first, though she felt wide awake after the nervous excitement of the evening and was convinced she would not sleep a wink. She was, in reality, exhausted and, with the sea air and the rhythm of the boat, drifted off almost immediately.

At four o'clock in the morning, she was awoken from a deep sleep by Spinet. She shivered. The night air was bitingly cold. Keeping her blanket wrapped around her shoulders, she joined Snipwicke at the tiller, while Spinet took her turn to rest.

"I trust the night has been uneventful?" she asked.

"A little too uneventful," said Snipwicke. "I had hoped for a fairer wind than this - we are doing not much above two knots."

"But surely we have nothing to worry about now," responded Hoglinda. "Why, by the time it is light again and they see we are gone, we shall have had a head start of... perhaps nine or even ten hours!"

"Well, yes, and, if only the wind will pick up a little, that should be enough to maintain our advantage. But at *this* speed... I fear we shall have covered barely twenty miles by the time the *Hogspur* comes after us."

"Is that not enough then?" asked Hoglinda.

"Not by any means! As you know, the *Hogspur* is much bigger and faster than the *Sea Urchin*. I reckon that, in a gentle breeze such as this, she could do three and a half knots to our two. And, when you consider that we have more than seventy miles to cover, an average difference of even just one knot can mean everything."

Hoglinda felt a little shiver run down her spines. But then a more positive thought occurred to her. "But if Mr Cutliss *does* catch us up," she began, "he still has to find us. And, if he believes we intend to report him - whether to the magistrate or the Governor, he must expect us to head for the east coast, must he not? And, as we are, in fact, heading west to Hog's Head Bay, might he not perhaps miss us altogether? Mr Snipwicke, how close would he have to be to spot us?"

"Oh, within about seven miles, I would say. So, yes, there's a good chance he will miss us, if he heads east. Perhaps I am being too gloomy. As you say, he may never even catch us up."

Snipwicke tried to sound cheerful, and no more was said on the subject. The rest of the night passed quietly. Now and then, they saw the distant lights of another vessel. On one occasion, as the lights grew closer and closer, Hoglinda half feared it must be the *Hogspur,* caught up with them already; but the vessel passed and she relaxed again.

At eight o'clock in the morning, Snipwicke finally settled down to get some sleep, leaving Spinet and Hoglinda in charge of his boat. They were under strict instructions to wake him if they had any difficulties of any sort or if anything happened or might be about to happen - or if they had any concerns at all. However, the day passed as quietly as the preceding night, and there was still no sign of the *Hogspur.*

When Snipwicke woke around noon, the wind was beginning to pick up a little. But it was too late to give him any reassurance. The *Hogspur* would undoubtedly have set sail by now and would benefit from the wind at least as much as the *Sea Urchin.*

On the second night (for such was the slowness of their progress), the weather suddenly took a turn for the worse. The wind grew strong, the sea rough, and Snipwicke called for all paws on deck. There would be no rest for anyone tonight. At around five o'clock in the morning, a streak of lightening lit up the sky in front of them. Hoglinda counted the seconds until the thunder clap: one...two...three. The lightening was just three miles away. The next time it was closer. Then the rain started, the first few drops suddenly followed by a torrential downpour. Though they had a canvas sheet on board for stringing between the masts as a shelter, they were too busy sailing the boat to take advantage of it. Hoglinda found it hard to think straight, with the wind in her face, the rain in her eyes, and the noise of the storm all around. Yet Snipwicke seemed calm enough. No doubt he had been through worse than this before. And, if he was still worried that his crew were not up to the situation, he did not show it.

As dawn broke, the lightening stopped, but the rain continued undiminished and the sky seemed scarcely any lighter. According to Snipwicke's calculations (though this was an inexact science in those days), they were now only about ten or twelve miles off the Isle of Needles. As he told the others, they should have been able to see the south-west coast by now. But, through the driving rain, they could scarcely see further than the ends of their noses.

Snipwicke gave the order to heave to and take a sounding. This would tell them the depth of the sea and help to confirm their position. So they turned into the wind and set the sails against one another to hold the boat as still as possible. Then Hoglinda hurled the lead-line into the sea. This was a long rope, with a lead weight attached to one end and coloured markers tied at intervals along its length. One after the other, the markers disappeared into the sea, dragged down by the lead weight until it had reached the bottom. A red marker was left suspended just above the surface: this told Hoglinda that the sea here was seventeen fathoms deep.

"By the mark seventeen!" she called.

Snipwicke stroked his chin. "Hmm, that sounds about right," he said to himself. Then he turned to his sister: "Spinet, take the tiller for me, while I check my chart."

"Aye, aye, sir," she said, as she took over the steering of the boat.

Snipwicke fetched his chart. Then, hunching over it to protect it from the rain, he pawed over the depth soundings he had previously marked upon it.

Hoglinda joined him. "Is that what you expected?" she asked.

"Yes, but it would be foolish to rely upon a single sounding or, indeed, to assume too much by it. Depths can be very misleading, Miss Hoglinda. If we are only a fraction more to the east than my calculations suggest, then we may also be a lot closer to the shore. So we'll take another sounding presently. In the meantime, we should continue slow and steady, until the air clears and we can see a little better."

No further explanation was necessary. To the east lay St Critter's Point, the southern tip of the island, whose rocks had wrecked many a vessel in better conditions than these. They reefed the sails and bore away cautiously. Then, after about five minutes, they hove to again. Hoglinda threw the lead-line into the sea once more; and once more the red 17-fathom marker was left suspended just above the surface. Satisfied now that his calculations were correct, Snipwicke gave the order to continue on the same course.

For the next few minutes, they continued slow and steady. Then, quite suddenly, the weather cleared. Ahead the sky was lighter now and the distant horizon was at last visible once more. Hoglinda looked back at the dark cloud they had just escaped from. The rain behind them was as torrential as ever; it seemed to rise like a grey mist from the sea. Thankfully, however, the cloud was moving eastwards and they were sailing north-west.

"Land-ho!" called Spinet suddenly. "Hog's Head Bay on the starboard bow! About ten miles off, north by north-west."

Hoglinda crouched down and peered under the mainsail. There it was at last, the Isle of Needles. Her relief at seeing her home again was immense. The return had taken so much longer than the outward trip - thirteen hours more, even though the wind had been behind them. But, of course, for most of the crossing the wind had been little more than a gentle breeze. Now she had to remind herself that they were not, in fact, home yet or safe. It was quite possible the *Hogspur* had already overtaken the *Sea Urchin* and was even now lying in wait for them. Looking through her spyglass, she scanned the horizon in every direction. A few miles to the west, there were two ships. One of them was a three-masted lugger, just like the *Hogspur,* and for a moment she feared the worst. Then she relaxed, for this lugger's sails were white; the *Hogspur's* were olive green.

With the improved visibility, Snipwicke gave the order to shake out the reefs. Then, with their sails full, they bore away north by north-west, on a direct course for Hog's Head Bay. As the island gradually grew closer, Hoglinda began to distinguish the white cliffs from the grassy downland behind. Above the island, the sky was a brighter grey, promising better weather. And behind them the rain-cloud was moving away, towards St Critter's Point. Hoglinda hoped no other vessels were caught beneath it; with such poor visibility, there would be a real risk of being dashed against the rocks.

But there *was* something. Through the veil of rain, it was hard to make her out, but the ship appeared to be heading north-east, with the rain-cloud chasing right after her. If only she would change direction - turn away from the rocks! Hoglinda need not have worried, for it soon became clear the ship would outrace the weather. But then, as the ship emerged from the rain, Hoglinda noticed she was a three-masted lugger and her sails were olive green. Hoglinda looked through her spyglass, and a chill ran down her spines. The *Hogspur* had caught up with them, after all.

"Mr Snipwicke, Spinet!" she shouted, moving down the boat hurriedly towards them. "It's the *Hogspur!* Off the starboard quarter - she's heading away from us but..." Before she could finish her sentence, the *Hogspur* began to turn: they had been spotted. For a moment, Hoglinda thought she saw a flicker of fear on Snipwicke's face, though the next moment it had gone.

"We'll head around the Needles Rocks, into the Strait," he said, sounding as calm and collected as ever. "It'll be busy there. Cutliss won't dare attack us with witnesses about... But let's not change course just yet. Let's make him think we're still hoping to come ashore in Hog's Head Bay. If we can lure him in past the headland, it will take him twice as long to leave again, with the wind against him."

"Aye, aye, sir," said Hoglinda and Spinet, as bravely as they could.

They resumed their positions by the mainsail and the mizzensail. And, for the next few minutes, the *Sea Urchin* continued on the same course, heading towards the westernmost part of Hog's Head Bay, just beyond the inn. Behind them the *Hogspur* was closing in fast, and soon there was barely four hundred yards separating the two vessels. Yet Snipwicke smiled to himself, for it was just as he had expected. The *Hogspur* was coming up on their landward side, hoping to cut them off and prevent them from coming ashore. To do so, she had had to sail further into the bay than the *Sea Urchin*. And now, with the headland straight ahead of her and the *Sea Urchin* to larboard, she herself was forced to bear away towards the shore.

"Stand by to luff up!" ordered Snipwicke. It was now the *Sea Urchin's* last chance to break away, before she too was caught behind the headland.

"Now!" he cried.

Hoglinda and Spinet hauled in the sheets, as Snipwicke pushed the tiller hard to starboard. The *Sea Urchin* turned - away from Hog's Head Bay and away from the *Hogspur*. They were now sailing very close to the wind and, with the cliffs and rocks immediately to starboard, there was little room to manoeuvre. But Snipwicke's deception had bought them time. The *Hogspur*, having sailed into the bay past the headland, would now have to beat to windward to leave

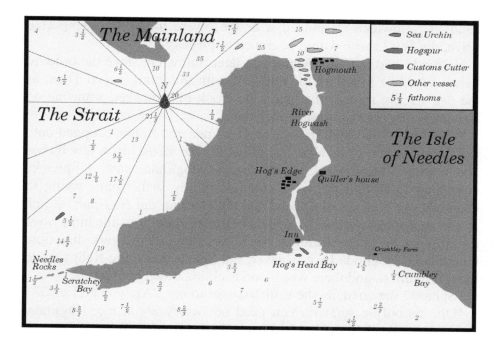

The map shows: The Mainland, The Strait, The Isle of Needles, Hogmouth, River Hogwash, Hog's Edge, Quiller's house, Inn, Crumbley Farm, Needles Rocks, Scratchey Bay, Hog's Head Bay, Crumbley Bay. Legend: Sea Urchin, Hogspur, Customs Cutter, Other vessel, $5\frac{1}{2}$ fathoms.

the bay - she would have to zigzag her way out, and this would lose her precious minutes. Furthermore, with her deep hull, she could not sail in the shallows like the *Sea Urchin*; she would have to head further out to sea in order to come around the headland safely.

By the time the *Hogspur* appeared back on the *Sea Urchin's* tail, Snipwicke had put a good half mile of water between them. But they were not safe yet. As the two vessels raced down the south-west coast, the gap between them began to close once more. By the time they reached Scratchey Bay, there was just three hundred yards between them. They were now well within firing range. With no other vessels nearby to deter an attack, Hoglinda feared the worst. The Strait, where they sought their safety, was so close and yet so far. For between them and it were the Needles Rocks, rising up from a dangerous underwater ledge, stretching almost a mile out to sea. To enter the Strait, they would have to sail right round it, but they had surely run out of time.

"Stand by to bear away!" shouted Snipwicke. "We're going to pass through the Needles."

For a moment, Hoglinda was horrified. Even for the *Sea Urchin,* with her flat-bottomed hull, such a manoeuvre was surely madness. Yet their situation was desperate. They seemed to be caught between the devil and the deep blue sea! And, if they did make it through, they would be safe: the *Hogspur* certainly could not follow. On the other

131

hand, if Snipwicke misjudged it or they were hit by an unexpected wave, the *Sea Urchin* would be ripped to pieces!

Hoglinda said nothing. A moment later Snipwicke gave the order to bear away. She loosened the mainsail with trembling paws. Then, as the *Sea Urchin* turned, she heard the crack of a musket; someone on board the *Hogspur* had just fired at them.

"Get down!" shouted Snipwicke. Hoglinda and Spinet dropped onto the floor of the boat as a second bullet hit the stern, just a few inches above the waterline. Looking back, Hoglinda saw Snipwicke crouching low, with the tiller clutched tightly in his paw, trying to keep one eye on the rocks ahead and the other on the *Hogspur* behind. It was an impossible task. Hoglinda began to crawl towards him, when a third shot hit the mizzenmast. Splinters flew off in every direction. One missed Hoglinda by a whisker; but Spinet was lying right next to the mizzenmast, and there was blood trickling down her face.

"Spinet!" she cried, as she shuffled over to her. "Are you all right?"

"Oh, 'tis only a scratch. You need not worry about me, Hoglinda. But Snipwicke..." Spinet looked back at her brother. "Why, if they get any closer... He is far too easy a target." She reflected for a moment and then remembered something. "You see that old sea chest over there? Snipwicke always keeps a couple of pistols in it. I say we give them a taste of their own medicine!"

132

"But I've never fired a weapon before in my life!" exclaimed Hoglinda. "Have you?"

"Not in anger," said Spinet, "but I know how to shoot. I can show you what to do."

Before Hoglinda could advise against it, Spinet had crawled off in the direction of the wooden chest. Hoglinda doubted that a pistol or two could have much effect against the *Hogspur* with her fourteen-strong crew. They probably had a musket apiece. But perhaps Spinet was right all the same. Perhaps it was better to go down fighting than surrender, for they could surely expect no mercy from Cutliss and his crew.

Having so reflected, Hoglinda was about to fetch the second pistol for herself, when she suddenly remembered the rocks ahead. So, leaving the defence of the *Sea Urchin* to Spinet, she instead made her way forward: from the bow, she would get a far better view of the rocks than was possible for Snipwicke at the stern.

As she began to move, several more shots smacked into the *Sea Urchin.* This time there was an answering shot from Spinet, followed by more firing from the *Hogspur,* and then a gasp of pain. She looked back to see that Snipwicke had been hit in the arm. Suppressing her

instincts to go and help him, she continued forward, just as there was another exchange of fire. But the next moment there was silence.

"I think they're turning away!" exclaimed Spinet. "Yes, they are! I can hardly believe it!"

Hoglinda was astonished, too. Had Spinet hit home? Was Cutliss injured perhaps? She could not believe they would be so cowardly as to flee from a single pistol. Getting up onto her knees, she peered over the bow to get a better view of the rocks ahead. And, as she looked out, the reason for the *Hogspur's* change of direction became all too clear.

"Ship ahoy!" she shouted, as loud as she could. "There's a Customs cutter off the larboard bow!"

The Customs ship was just beyond the Needles Rocks and, until a moment ago, had been hidden from view. Snipwicke reacted immediately. With contraband on board, the *Sea Urchin* would have to flee like the *Hogspur*.

"Ready about!" he called, his voice as calm and steady as ever, despite the terrible pain in his arm.

Hoglinda and Spinet jumped to their feet and resumed their positions. "Ready!" they responded.

"Lee ho!" shouted Snipwicke, as he pushed the tiller hard to starboard.

Spinet pulled the mizzensail across, and Hoglinda dipped the mainsail; then, as the *Sea Urchin* turned across the wind, she hoisted it back up the other side of the mast. This manoeuvre brought them almost full circle, so they were now pointing east-south-east - back the way they had come.

The deadly battle between the *Hogspur* and the *Sea Urchin* was forgotten now, as both smuggling luggers fled before the Customs cutter. But it was an unequal race: the *Hogspur* was not only the faster of the two luggers, she was also the farthest away. It seemed all too likely the *Sea Urchin* would be caught - leaving the *Hogspur* to get clean away. Hoglinda watched anxiously as the Customs cutter gained on them. The cutter's sudden appearance had saved them from near-certain death. Yet Hoglinda feared that imprisonment would be little better; and the disgrace of a public trial would be worse still.

As they sailed across Hog's Head Bay, the beach seemed tantalisingly close, but yet again a landing there was impossible. In a deep bay such as this, the Customs cutter could follow them almost to the shore and fire upon them as they disembarked. So instead they headed a little further along the coast to Crumbley Bay. Here the sea was shallow and there were dangerous ledges, which were just about passable by the *Sea Urchin*, with her flat bottom, but not by the Customs cutter.

As they approached Crumbley Bay, the cutter fired a warning shot. It was a signal for them to heave-to; but Snipwicke had no intention of allowing them on board, with all the contraband he was carrying.

"What shall we do?" asked Spinet, who was reluctant to fire upon officers of the law.

"We ignore it," said Snipwicke, "but you need to get ready to throw the tubs overboard. We shan't be able to carry them away today, as there will be no one to meet us."

Hoglinda and Spinet set to work, attaching four tubs to a ready-prepared rope, with an anchor tied to either end and three stones along its length. When released, the tubs would sink straight to the bottom, out of sight of the Customs. Later on, when the coast was clear, they could be collected with a grappling hook. As Hoglinda and Spinet hurriedly secured the tubs, the Customs fired another shot. It landed with a splash just a couple of yards short of the *Sea Urchin*.

"That was the second warning shot," said Snipwicke. "The law requires them to fire two, you see. So keep your heads down now. Next time they will be trying to hit us."

Hoglinda and Spinet kept their heads as low as possible, as they secured the last eight tubs to two more ropes. When the Customs fired again, the first shot ripped right through the mizzensail. The second pierced the very tub which Hoglinda had just finished securing. She gasped with the shock, her paws shaking as she watched the brandy gush out onto the floor of the boat. Then she pulled herself together. It was not important: the rest of the tubs were still intact and so was she.

It was now time to head for the shore. Hoglinda and Spinet let out the sails and Snipwicke pushed the tiller to starboard until they were running before the wind. Hoglinda looked back, fearing and expecting the Customs cutter would do just the same - for they were not yet in the shallows and could still be followed. Yet the cutter's course did not alter.

Hoglinda looked through her spyglass. "Why, they aren't following us!" she exclaimed. "No, I do believe they are going after the *Hogspur* instead!"

"Stands to reason," said Snipwicke, smiling to himself, in spite of the intense pain in his arm. "The *Hogspur* is the greater prize and, unlike us, she cannot come ashore. Her only chance is to out-race the Customs cutter or fight. They know it, and the Customs know it."

"But why do the Customs have to choose between us?" asked Hoglinda, hardly daring to believe that Snipwicke could be right. "They could launch their boat; then, while the cutter pursued the *Hogspur,* the boat could come after us. I mean, if the *Sea Urchin* can make it safely into Crumbley Bay, then surely any ship's boat can."

"Not so, Miss Hoglinda. You forget they do not know the bay and its rocks and ledges as I do. It takes local knowledge and years of experience to bring a boat ashore here; and that they do not have."

"So we are safe then?"

"Not quite yet – when we are past the rocks. Indeed, we are approaching them right now. Lower the mainsail, if you please - we'll come in under the mizzen. Then stand by with the tubs."

Hoglinda and Spinet pulled down the mainsail. Then, just before they reached the rocks, they released the tubs - on the shoreward side, out of view of the Customs. Snipwicke examined the cliffs carefully in order to get his bearing. Then he pushed the tiller a fraction to starboard and straightened it again. Coming in at an angle and as slowly as possible, he guided the *Sea Urchin* into a gap in the rocks. Hoglinda glanced over the side, but the rocks were invisible, hidden by

the swirl of sand and surf. There were, indeed, few hedgehogs who could have brought them safely through this.

"Spinet!" called Snipwicke. "Miss Hoglinda! Get ready to turn the boat."

Spinet was already crouching on the starboard side, poised to jump out; her jacket, boots and stockings and even her outer petticoats were off. Hoglinda hastily removed her own. Then, catching the sound of distant gunfire, she glanced back. The cutter was catching up with the *Hogspur* – and it looked as though they were going to fight it out! She hardly knew who she wanted to win; but this was no matter for her. She moved behind Spinet, hoping fervently that the water would not be too deep. When this was all over, she told herself, she really must learn to swim.

"Now!" barked Snipwicke.

Spinet and Hoglinda jumped into the water. It was well above their waists and freezing! Hoglinda grabbed the side of the boat and, together with Spinet, quickly swung the *Sea Urchin* round between the breaking waves, until the stern was facing the shore. Snipwicke pulled up the tiller and jumped out as the boat made contact with the beach. Then the three hedgehogs - with just five working paws between them - heaved the lugger up the beach until they could take her no further.

"Whatever shall we do?" asked Hoglinda, for the *Sea Urchin* was still half in the water. "If we leave her here, she'll have floated away by the time we come back."

"No, she'll be all right here for a good few hours yet," said Snipwicke. "The tide's going out, you see. But I confess I *am* concerned about the Customs coming back. It isn't just the cargo I stand to lose. If they can prove I've been smuggling, they'll destroy my boat. So, if you do not object, I would like to call at Crumbley Farm on the way. The farmer there's an old friend of the family. I can ask him and his sons to move the *Sea Urchin* for me. It needn't delay us long, for the farm's just above the chine here - though I think a few minutes in front of a warm fire would be sensible. January is no time to be walking about in wet clothes."

Hoglinda and Spinet agreed wholeheartedly. Putting their dry clothes back on over their wet clothes was not a pleasant experience. When fully dressed again, Hoglinda pulled down the mizzensail and unloaded their bags. Spinet tended to her brother, tying a tourniquet around his wounded arm, to prevent further loss of blood, and putting his arm in a sling. Then she helped Hoglinda dismantle the masts; and, when the Customs cutter had finally disappeared from sight, they unloaded the remaining cargo - two packets of lace and three crates of tea.

"We'll bury the rest of the cargo," said Snipwicke, fetching a spade from the boat. He took them fifty yards down the beach and then stopped. "Here, this will do," he said, pointing to an expanse of dry sand beneath the cliff. "Can you see the high water mark there? That's where we need to dig - or rather, Spinet, where *you* need to dig, for I am afraid it is beyond me in my present state. But I will stand guard - and Miss Hoglinda, too, if you don't mind? Spinet, would you give Miss Hoglinda your pistol?"

"Oh, no, Mr Snipwicke!" said Hoglinda, shrinking back a little. "I have no idea how to handle a gun. In any case, I would much prefer to dig."

So saying, she took the spade from him and immediately set to work. It was, in fact, much harder and much less fun than she had expected - digging large holes in dry sand is not an easy thing to do. Very soon her back was aching, but she pressed on. When the crates were buried, she went about the beach, scooping up pawfuls of pebbles and seaweed. She then arranged these carefully over the disturbed area, so that it was indistinguishable from the rest of the beach.

Standing back to examine the effect, she felt a curious sense of achievement and even pleasure, despite her aching back.

But it was time to go. Picking up their bags, the three hedgehogs set off down the beach. They walked in silence, each of them wrapped up in their own thoughts. Hoglinda was dreading the confrontation with her cousin. She felt as though *she* were the traitor. Quiller had done so much for her. Yet she had gone to Snipwicke behind his back. She had eavesdropped on his conversations, read his letters and lied to him.

Spinet's anxiety was for her brother with that bullet lodged in his arm. He had lost a lot of blood and needed a physician urgently. Yet the meeting with Quiller could not be delayed; and she knew perfectly well that Snipwicke would never let Hoglinda confront her cousin alone.

Snipwicke, meanwhile, was trying to ignore the pain in his arm. He was determined not to let Hoglinda down. She had shown such courage - not just physical, but moral courage, too. It could not have been easy, taking a stand against her own cousin - a cousin she clearly cared for, traitor though he was. And naturally she was anxious to protect Quiller's young hoglets, who were of course innocent of their father's crimes. Yet, despite all her worries - despite everything, Hoglinda had put her country first. She had put right before wrong.

It was a little over three miles to Quiller's house - over the cliff tops, then inland along the River Hogwash to Hog's Edge. Snipwicke was exhausted by the walk and, as they were approaching Quiller's house, he leant upon his sister's arm. In the garden, they found Quillemina and Quillip playing, watched over by Pinafore. The two hoglets were happy and laughing. It sent a chill of dread down Hoglinda's spines.

"Hogwinda!" cried little Quillip, spotting her. Quillemina looked up from their game; and the two hoglets ran to greet their cousin. Hoglinda had been away just five days, but to them it seemed like an age. For Hoglinda herself, who feared this might be the last time she ever saw them and knowing she would be the cause, the warmth of their greeting brought only pain.

"Quillemina! Quip!" she said, trying not to cry. "How are you? Were you good while I was away?"

The two hoglets responded that they had been very good indeed. Then they grabbed Hoglinda by the paw, hoping she would join in their game.

"I'm sorry, not now," she said. "Later perhaps. I must speak to your father first."

"Oh, but Mr Quiller be out, ma'am," interjected Pinafore. "He wasn't expecten' you back so soon... as you hadn't sent no word." She looked at Snipwicke and Spinet suspiciously. "And he wasn't expecten' no visitors, neither."

"No, indeed, Pinafore. My business was concluded sooner than I expected. Do you know when Mr Quiller will be back?"

"No, ma'am, that I don't."

"I see. Well, we shall just have to wait for him then. In the meantime, as you can see, Mr Snipwicke here needs a physician. Go and fetch Dr Lancet, and tell him to come immediately."

"Yes, ma'am." Pinafore curtseyed. Then, putting down her basket of laundry, she rushed off down the garden path.

Hoglinda took her friends into the parlour, where they were met by Mrs Brush, who offered them some refreshment. When they declined, she left them to themselves and disappeared back off down the corridor to the kitchen. Though alone now, they waited in silence, fearing even to talk among themselves in case they were overheard. Hoglinda paced about the room just as she had done a fortnight ago, when waiting for the *Hogspur's* return; but then at least she had been looking forward to seeing her cousin. She glanced at Mr Snipwicke, who did not look at all well. Where on earth was that physician?

The clock on the wall ticked loudly, as though to emphasize the slow passage of time. They waited ten minutes... then twenty... After almost an hour, Dr Lancet finally arrived. Hoglinda hoped he would not recognize her from their meeting at the Hog's Head Inn, when she had been in disguise and going under the name of Hoggin. Happily, his attention was focussed on his patient, just as it had been before.

Removing the tourniquet from around Snipwicke's arm, Dr Lancet examined the wound. Then he placed his paw on Snipwicke's forehead. "Hmm. Just as I thought," he said. "You are running a fever, sir. I need to remove that bullet now. I have all my equipment with me. So, Miss Hoglinda, if you will have a room made ready, I will perform the operation straightaway."

"Of course," said Hoglinda. "Is there anything else you need?"

"A bottle of brandy to dull the pain, if you please."

"But you cannot mean to perform the operation here!" protested Snipwicke weakly. He would have much preferred to have undergone the ordeal in his own home or at least at a friend's house; but the weakness of his voice only demonstrated the urgency of the situation.

"Oh, I am sure Mr Quiller won't mind," said Dr Lancet. "Will he, Miss Hoglinda? Indeed, this will not be the first time I've attended to a wounded hedgehog in his house."

Snipwicke appealed to Hoglinda. "You must surely see this is impossible! What if your cousin were to arrive in the middle of the operation?"

"In the middle of what operation?"

It was Quiller who spoke. He had just walked through the door. Silence fell upon the room so that you might have heard a pin drop. Though they had been expecting him - had, indeed, come on purpose to see him, he had somehow managed to take them all by surprise.

Hoglinda pulled herself together: "I am so glad you are come home, Quiller. The operation we speak of is one to remove a bullet from Mr Snipwicke's arm. Dr Lancet says it should be done as soon as possible."

"Well, if that is what Dr Lancet recommends, then it must be done." There was a coldness in Quiller's voice that sent a shiver down Hoglinda's spines. Without further enquiry, Quiller went into the hallway and called Mrs Brush and Pinafore into the parlour.

143

"Dr Lancet here," he said to them, when they appeared, "needs to perform an operation upon Mr Snipwicke. Show them into the dining room and prepare the room as Dr Lancet directs... Oh, and fetch Mr Snipwicke a bottle of brandy. I imagine he will need it."

The housekeeper and the maid disappeared and, with a gesture of his paw, Quiller indicated that Dr Lancet and Snipwicke should follow them. When they had gone, Quiller turned to Spinet.

"I do not believe I have had the pleasure," he said graciously.

"This is Spinet," said Hoglinda hesitantly. "Mr Snipwicke's sister."

"How d'you do?" said Quiller with a little bow. "Now, Miss Spinet, I am sure you will want to be with your brother at such a time as this. Please do not let me detain you."

Spinet glanced anxiously at Hoglinda. "Oh, I... I think they can manage without *me*."

"But I insist," said Quiller.

He took Spinet by the paw and led her gently to the door. When she had gone, he closed the door behind her. Quiller and Hoglinda were now alone.

"Well?" said Quiller.

Hoglinda felt weak at the knees. Somehow, without Snipwicke and Spinet by her side, all her courage seemed to disappear. She sat down, but the words failed her.

"I think I am due an explanation," said Quiller. "Let us start with what Mr Snipwicke is doing in my house. What exactly is the nature of your relationship with Mr Snipwicke?"

"We are friends!" said Hoglinda defensively. "As are his sister and I. The reason they are - " She broke off mid-sentence. She had hardly noticed it at first, but boiling up inside her was a new feeling - anger. The way Quiller had spoken to her just now was not to be borne. Why should she have to defend her actions to *him* - a traitor to his country?

"No," she said, standing up. There was a steely edge to her voice now, which made Quiller start. "I believe it is you, cousin, who must defend yourself. I know all about your agreement with Monsieur Espinon. I know that you have been spying for the Furzish government."

Quiller did not speak, but his astonishment was plain to see. Warming to her theme, Hoglinda began to pace about the room again.

"I know of the Furzish plan to invade the Isle of Needles," she said, "and that you have been helping Monsieur Espinon with that plan. I know that you have recruited local pilots to guide the invasion fleet ashore; that you have shown Monsieur Espinon around our island and

144

passed him information about the military depot, the hospital, where to find food for the Furzish invaders, timber supplies for their ships... Need I go on?"

Quiller fought against the rising tide of fear which threatened to engulf him. He had to think - and think fast. If Hoglinda knew all this, did Snipwicke also know? But Snipwicke would surely have reported him to the authorities...

"Well, cousin," said Hoglinda. She folded her arms and looked him directly in the eye. "I think I am due an explanation, am I not? Why are you working for our Furzish enemies?"

Quiller got up and walked to the window. Looking out, he could see Quillemina and Quillip playing in the garden. A shiver ran down his spines. What had he done? Treachery was punishable by death. Were the two hoglets now to become orphans? Would they have to live the rest of their lives under the shadow of their father's disgrace? But Hoglinda had asked him for an explanation. Now, surely, was his chance to win her over.

"I do it for liberty," he said, standing tall. "For the liberty of the colonies. I assist the Furzish, and they assist the rebels."

His reply came as no surprise to Hoglinda, of course - and it did nothing to lessen her anger. "Their liberty!" she exclaimed. "Are they not free enough already? Why, as subjects of the king, they enjoy the same freedoms as you and I!"

"You are mistaken," said Quiller. "Unlike us, they have no one in Parliament to speak for them. How can they be free when they are taxed without representation? Money is taken from them - but they have no say over it. That is not freedom; it is tyranny!"

"Tyranny!" cried Hoglinda. "It would hardly be practical to send Members of Parliament over the ocean. How could they possibly represent the colonies at such a distance?"

"You make my point for me, cousin. It is impractical. And for that reason, the colonies must be set free."

Hoglinda bit her lip. If only her father were present, he would know what to say. Then she remembered his last letter, in which he had explained that not all the colonists were rebels. Quite a few were loyal to the king and some even fought under her father's command. "And what of the Loyalists?" she asked. "Those who fight for their king? What of *their* freedom to choose?"

"They are fools!" said Quiller scornfully. "Frightened fools, who are afraid to stand on their own two feet."

"But the rebels don't stand on their own two feet, do they?" she responded. "Why, they would already have lost the war, were it not for Furzish arms and money. And now, while the rebels demand their own freedom, they are busy planning a secret alliance with the Furzish king! A king whose subjects would rejoice at the freedoms the rebels already enjoy. *And*," she said, getting to the point at last, "when the Furzish invade the Isle of Needles, will you cry 'Liberty!' then?"

For the first time, Quiller looked uncomfortable. "Well, it will only be for the duration of the war," he said defensively. "The Furzish want to defeat Great Bristlin, not to conquer her. In any case, once they have invaded the mainland, they will have little need of our island. Most of their troops will depart and very probably we shall barely notice their presence at all."

"Is that what Monsieur Espinon has told you?" asked Hoglinda. "Then he has been lying to you. The Furzish intend to *expel* the islanders - *all* of us. I know it because I heard him say so himself."

"This is absurd!" said Quiller, though she heard the doubt in his voice. "How could you have heard him?"

"Quiller, these last few days, I have been in Gruntsey, with Mr Snipwicke and Miss Spinet. I followed Monsieur Espinon and heard him talking with the Furzish spy they want you to report to. Her name - in case it interests you - is Madame Hérispionne. She is the wife of the harbour master."

Quiller looked at her with horror. He told himself she must be lying. After all, she had lied about going to her father's house. Yet her words had the ring of truth about them. In fact, much of what she said he knew to be true; and there was nothing which he knew to be untrue. Besides, what reason could she have to lie now?

"Why are you telling me this?" he asked at last. "Why are you not gone to the authorities with this information?"

"Because I do not want to see you hang," she said, "and because I believed - and told Mr Snipwicke - that, once you knew the truth - the full truth - you would want to have nothing more to do with Monsieur Espinon."

Quiller looked away, unable to meet her eye. Her words had moved him deeply. If only he could have turned back the clock...

"Well?" she said.

"It is no good, Hoglinda," he said at last. "Espinon has other connections here now. He doesn't need *me*. Any one of us could report to this Furzish spy - to Madame Hérispionne. Indeed, I am not entirely sure that Espinon trusts me any more. I rather think he keeps me on because he wishes to keep an eye on me."

"I know," said Hoglinda. "That is why you mustn't break off contact. You must report to Madame Hérispionne, just as you promised, but give her false information."

"I doubt very much that would work. If I suddenly tell her the island's so well defended that an invasion would be bound to fail, she will hardly be likely to believe me."

"Well, yes, of course - if you were to tell her *that*, but you can be more subtle, I am sure. What is more, if you are clever about it, you might even be able to glean a little information from *her*. Her very questions should tell you something."

Quiller was silent for a moment, while he considered Hoglinda's proposal. But, before he could answer, there was a commotion at the front door.

"Mr Quiller! Mr Quiller!"

It was Cutliss! So the *Hogspur* had fought off the Customs cutter!

"Please, sir," they heard Pinafore say, "if you'll jest wait a moment, I'll let the master know you be here."

"No, there's no time to be lost!" said Cutliss. "Where is he?"

The door to the parlour burst open, and Cutliss rushed in with a pistol grasped in his paw. Through the open doorway, Hoglinda could

see two members of his crew, who were also armed and seemed to be guarding the front entrance.

"Mr Quiller, sir!" said Cutliss, closing the parlour door behind him. "You've been - " Then, seeing Hoglinda, he broke off. "I see," he said. "So Miss Hoglinda has made it here afore us. Perhaps then you know already that she has betrayed you?"

"I know that my cousin has uncovered our secret," said Quiller. "More than that, she has revealed the true intentions of Espinon and his compatriots." He sighed. "It seems they have deceived us for, when they invade the Isle of Needles, they intend to expel the entire population of the island."

"Bilge! Hogwash!" said Cutliss. "Forgive me, Mr Quiller, but why should we believe her?"

"Why should I make it up?" she protested.

"To save yourself!" he snarled.

"This is insufferable!" cried Hoglinda, needled by the deep injustice of the accusation. "I came back to save my *cousin*, not myself. I could very easily have gone to the authorities with this information, but I chose not to."

Cutliss reflected for a moment. Then his expression hardened. "Sir," he said, ignoring Hoglinda again, "suppose she does speak the truth, think of the hold this information gives her over us. Why, she's got us over a barrel! Are we to live forever under her power? Not I, for one!"

As he spoke, he raised his paw and pointed his pistol straight at Hoglinda.

"No!" shouted Quiller, placing himself between Cutliss and his cousin. "Put down your gun at once, Mr Cutliss! Do you hear?"

Cutliss did not move but barked at his hench-hogs to come into the parlour. "Razzer! Scart! In here!" A second later they appeared.

"Take Miss Hoglinda for a walk along the cliffs," said Cutliss, "and see she takes a tumble… I think that's rather fitting, don't you, Miss Hoglinda? We all know how you do love to walk along the cliff tops."

Hoglinda stared at him in terror and disbelief. She knew he had never really liked her and knew him to be ruthless; but she had never supposed him capable of such cold-blooded murder. Before she knew it, Razzer had seized Quiller. Then Scart grabbed her by the arm and started dragging her towards the door.

"No!" she screamed. "Get your paws off me!"

"Let her go!" barked Quiller.

"I'm sorry, Mr Quiller," said Cutliss, "but I cannot oblige you. Of course, if she'll tell us where Mr Snipwicke is, we can arrange something quick and painless for her."

"No need for that, Mr Cutliss. I am here."

Cutliss felt the end of a pistol in his back. Having heard Hoglinda's scream, Snipwicke had leapt from the operating table and come rushing to the parlour with Spinet. They were both armed.

"Put down your weapons!" ordered Snipwicke. There was nothing about his manner to suggest the pain he was in or any dullness brought on by the fever or the brandy.

"Why should we?" asked Razzer. "We outnumber and outgun you!"

"Well, let us put that question to Mr Cutliss, shall we?"

"Do as he says," said Cutliss, scowling, for he knew that he would certainly be killed in any exchange of fire.

"Very sensible," said Snipwicke. "Now, Spinet, collect their weapons, if you please."

She took their weapons; and Hoglinda and Quiller were released.

"What are you going to do with them, Mr Snipwicke?" asked Hoglinda, nervously. Thankful though she was for her rescue, she remained fearful of how this would all end.

"That partly depends upon what your cousin has to say. Well, Quiller? I am sure you will have heard our proposal by now?"

"Yes," said Quiller, "that I have." He was silent for a moment, as though still considering what answer he would give; but it was the pain of his decision that made him slow to respond.

"Well?" said Snipwicke again.

Quiller sighed. "I accept." So saying, he offered Hoglinda his paw to seal their agreement. But instead - much to his surprise - she threw her arms around him in joy.

"So I shall only have three passengers then," said Snipwicke, smiling - it pleased him to see Hoglinda so happy.

"What do you mean?" growled Cutliss.

"I am taking the three of you to Pawsmouth to join the navy. You were so keen that my crew and I should join, I thought I should return the favour. When the war comes, Mr Cutliss, you will be fighting on the correct side – *for* your country and *against* the Furzish."

Hoglinda, on hearing this clever solution, breathed a sigh of relief.

"You can't force me," said Cutliss.

"So long as I have this pistol pointed at your back, I can," said Snipwicke, "and, I assure you, I shall be escorting you all the way to the door."

"Mr Quiller!" said Cutliss. "Surely you're not going to let 'em get away with this! I'm on *your* side!"

Hoglinda could hear the hurt and the anger in his voice. For a moment she wondered whether he might now betray Quiller to the authorities out of revenge. But that would be risking his own neck, and she doubted very much he would do that.

"I'm sorry," said Quiller, heavy of heart, "but you can see I am powerless here. Besides, you made a grave mistake when you threatened to kill my cousin. I think you should be grateful that you have come out of this with your lives... I know that I am."

Quiller turned to Hoglinda, but she was looking out of the window. She was watching Quillemina and Quillip playing innocently in the garden, unaware of just how close they had come to losing their father. And they were not the only ones who would have felt Quiller's loss. So many hedgehogs in the neighbourhood and beyond relied upon him - the very same hedgehogs he had been about to betray. And, though his ignorance of the plan to expel them lessened his crime in Hoglinda's eyes, she suspected that others would not have been quite so forgiving. Thankfully none would ever discover his treachery now.

Hoglinda felt a surge of pride, as she reflected that it was she and her friends who had done this for him. They had saved Quiller, not only from death and disgrace, but from himself. And, somehow, it had been the making of her. When she had arrived in Hog's Head Bay, almost a year ago, she had been naïve: she had seen everything in black and white and been far too quick to judge the actions of others. Since then, however, she had learned so much. She had learned that life was complicated and confusing - but that it could be exciting, too. She had learned that you always had a choice, even if sometimes it was a choice between two evils; then, of course, the trick was to work out the lesser of the two. Not that she had all the answers - no hedgehog does. But that, of course, was precisely the point.

Quiller kept his word. Though his heart remained with the rebels in the colonies, he made no further attempt to support their Furzish allies. On the contrary, he now actively sought to prevent a Furzish invasion, by passing false information to Hérispionne, just as he had promised Hoglinda he would do. The exact details of this false information were worked out and agreed in advance by Hoglinda, Snipwicke, Spinet and Quiller himself. The four hedgehogs were careful not to go overboard with the tales they made up, not wanting to arouse Hérispionne's suspicions. So they kept to the truth as much as possible; but every piece of news likely to encourage an invasion was downplayed or ignored, while every discouraging piece of news was seized upon, exaggerated and embellished.

So, when a company of soldiers arrived on the Isle of Needles to reinforce the small garrison already present, Quiller promptly sailed to Gruntsey and reported to Hérispionne that an entire battalion had arrived - ten times the real number. When some minor repairs were carried out at Scratchdown Fort, Quiller told her the fort had been strengthened and extended. And, when the new Collector of Customs bought an extra cutter for patrolling the Strait between the island and the mainland, Quiller claimed the cutter was intended for the south coast, where the invaders were due to land.

Hoglinda, Snipwicke, Quiller and Spinet came together to discuss all of this once a week at Bristlestone Mill. Their meetings were, at first, conducted in a very business-like manner. They would discuss at length whatever news they had heard or read in the paper and how this might be used. But sometimes there was no news. Then they would relax and talk about other things; and either Spinet or Hoglinda would play a little music on the harpsichord. Over time the four hedgehogs grew very close. The past was not forgotten, of course. That was impossible, particularly in view of the purpose of their meetings. But Snipwicke had long since forgiven Quiller for his previous behaviour towards him; and Quiller, for his own part, had given up the sharp business practices which had caused them to quarrel in the first place. As for the rebellion in the colonies, it was not often mentioned between them. When it was, they generally agreed to disagree...

"So it has happened," said Snipwicke, one evening late in February, as they all sat in his parlour. He tossed a newspaper onto the table.

"Have you seen this? The Furzish have recognized the rebels' independence."

"Well, it was only a matter of time," said Quiller, who was unable to hide his pleasure.

"Hmm," said Snipwicke. "Well, I suppose, at least one of us is happy about it."

Quiller shrugged his shoulders. "I cannot tell a lie."

But, of course, they all knew that Quiller was perfectly capable of telling a lie. Hoglinda glanced at Snipwicke and was surprised to see him break into a smile.

"My dear Quiller," said Snipwicke, "if that be the case, you are not much use to us!"

Quiller looked surprised himself. Then he laughed - and they all laughed. Hoglinda thought how wonderful it was that these three hedgehogs, for whom she cared so much, could all be such good friends now despite their differences! It wanted only the return of her father to make her happiness complete.

"Ahem." She coughed, and the laughter subsided. "I have some other news to report," she said, with a significant look. There was silence. She looked round at her friends as though challenging them to guess her news.

"Well?" said Spinet eagerly.

"It's my father," began Hoglinda, with a broad smile. "He is returning from the colonies on leave! I only received his letter yesterday, but it's dated the 12th of December, so I expect him any day!"

"Any day?" said Spinet, who was a little taken aback. "Oh! Well, this is excellent news - I am so very happy for you, Hoglinda."

"We are all happy for you," said Snipwicke earnestly, "but we shall miss you."

"Miss me?"

"You will be returning to your home in Brambling, will you not? From such a distance I fear it will be impossible for you to attend our meetings."

"Oh!" said Hoglinda, who had not thought of that. "Well, it is *quite* far, I suppose... but not impossible. I could perhaps stay with Quiller from time to time. That is," she added, turning to her cousin, "if you are not tired of having me in your home?"

"Hmm?" said Quiller distractedly. His thoughts were clearly elsewhere. "Oh! No, no, of course I am not. I would be delighted to have you stay with me - as would the hoglets."

"Thank you. That is very kind of you, Quiller... But only if you are sure."

"Of course I am sure, Hoglinda. Nothing could please me more, so you must come as often as you like."

Hoglinda watched her cousin with concern. He had responded without hesitation and she was persuaded he meant what he had said; but she could see he was ill at ease.

"Quiller, is something troubling you? Is it my father's return?"

"Well... I..." He seemed unwilling to explain.

"So it *is* that! Quiller, I promise, you have nothing to fear: I shall not tell papa about your Furzish connections. Indeed, I think it would be very unfair on him, if I were to do so. For it would put him in a very difficult position. As an officer of the Bristlish Navy, he would feel it his duty to report you. Yet to do so would break his heart - and mine."

At this, Quiller relaxed visibly, and Hoglinda knew she had guessed correctly. "Thank you," he said, squeezing her paw affectionately. Then he turned to the others: "Thank you, *all* of you - I know I do not deserve such friendship as this."

"Probably not," said Snipwicke, as he leaned back in his chair with an amused smile. "Yet you have it all the same."

154

"Indeed you do," said Spinet, with such feeling that Quiller could not have hoped for more.

* * *

Admiral Hoglander arrived on the Isle of Needles just two days later. Being eager to see his daughter as soon as possible, he fetched her from Quiller's house the very same day. Hoglinda was overjoyed to see him and to find him looking so well - indeed, he seemed extraordinarily unchanged by the war. The admiral, however, found that his daughter *had* changed a great deal. She appeared to have grown up in his absence. She was certainly more sure of herself and seemed always to be busy about something or other - though quite what she was busy about was not clear, for she did not tell him. Neither did she have much to say about her time at Quiller's house and what she had done there. She had been happy, she said. Quiller had been good company, the hoglets had been delightful and she had made a couple of new friends over in Bristlestone, but she said very little about them. It was also evident that she had walked about the countryside a great deal and had come to love it as much as anywhere around Brambling. Yet, when the admiral asked whether she had done many sketches or paintings, she claimed that she had not had the time for it. All in all, she seemed to have developed quite an air of mystery about her - quite unlike the daughter he had left behind when he had sailed to the colonies all those months ago.

Several weeks passed before Hoglinda finally got up the courage to tell her father a little more of the truth. She had, of course, no intention of betraying Quiller's darkest secret, but she knew that she could not keep her own smuggling activities to herself forever.

"This is a very good wine, papa," she said one evening, by way of an opening. "I suppose it is one of Quiller's."

"Whatever do you mean?" said the admiral.

"Oh, come now, papa! I could hardly live with my cousin for the best part of a year and not know how he spends his time."

"I see... Well, I confess I was a little worried about that, but I did ask Quiller to keep it to himself."

"Oh, you mustn't blame Quiller. He did his very best, I can assure you. No, I discovered the truth all by myself."

"You did, did you? Well, I suppose it was foolish of me to expect otherwise... And perhaps it is just as well that you should understand a

155

little of the ways of the world. But you must not think too badly of your cousin, Hoglinda - or of your poor old papa, for that matter. Why, it is harder to buy a bottle of wine that *has* had the tax paid upon it than not! Indeed, there is hardly a hedgehog on the island who is not -"

"I know, papa," interrupted Hoglinda. "Almost everyone on the island is involved in smuggling, one way or another - and that includes me."

"Heavens above, Hoglinda!" exclaimed the admiral, who was horrified. "I have to say I am most gravely disappointed."

"But why? If you do not disapprove of smuggling - but indeed actively support it by buying your wines from your nephew, how then can you object to *my* involvement in it?"

"Because it is unfeminine - and far too dangerous."

"Pshaw!" said Hoglinda. "Everyone else takes risks and has their fun. I think it very unfair that I should be forced to stay at home and do nothing."

The admiral eyed his daughter sternly. "What exactly has been the nature of your involvement?"

"Well," she said, fiddling with her knife, "I invested a little of my money in his last smuggling run..."

"And?"

"And I carried a few messages for Quiller..."

"Are you sure that was all you carried?"

"Well, the odd wineskin or a packet of lace now and then. But really, papa, that was all. Quiller never allowed me to meet the *Hogspur* when she returned from a run."

"I should hope not!" said the admiral. "Why, it is bad enough that you were carrying contraband for him. And, as for your investing your allowance - the allowance that you get from *me*... I shall have to have words with Quiller."

"Please don't, papa! It was my idea, not his. Indeed, I do believe he only agreed to my being involved, because he was too afraid to refuse me. You see, when I first found out about his smuggling, I did disapprove - a great deal, in fact. I even tried to scuttle the *Hogspur,* to put a stop to his activities."

"Good heavens, Hoglinda!" exclaimed the admiral, who could hardly believe his ears. "You tried to sink the *Hogspur!*"

"Oh, but I did not succeed. And, once he explained why he smuggled, I was very glad I had not, for I then began to see his point of view. But, after such a poor beginning, I think he only felt safe once I was just as involved as he was."

"I see... Well, what is done is done, I suppose," said the admiral, trying to be philosophical about it. "At least you are safe and back home with me now. We shall say no more about it - though you must first promise me that you will have nothing more to do with Quiller's smuggling business."

"Oh, you need not worry, papa. For what can I do living here? Aside from investing my allowance, and I promise not to do that again. As for the rest... Well, I suppose it is over now - but, I'm sorry, I cannot *promise* you that."

Admiral Hoglander was shocked by his daughter's refusal to obey him. But then he reflected on it. He had been away for almost a year, and she had naturally become used to her independence. Could he really expect her to give that up now? Besides, her smuggling days were probably over anyway, as she said. So why push the point? The last thing he wanted was to make her regret his return. So he said no more about it, and the subject was not brought up again.

Hoglinda's refusal to make the promise her father sought masked her uncertain feelings on the subject. She had begun to have doubts some time ago about her involvement in the Trade, having seen how easily it could lead to violence. Yet she missed the excitement. She also missed her cousins and her new friends, and wanted so very much to carry on going to the weekly meetings between Quiller, Snipwicke and Spinet. But how to justify such frequent visits to the other side of the island? She did not want to lie to her father but neither could she tell him the full truth about his nephew.

It was as she sat down to play the harpsichord that evening, that the answer came to her. The one thing she had really missed in Quiller's house was music - a home without it seemed somehow incomplete. But this was easily put right. For what could be more natural than a gift to the hoglets, by way of a thank you to their father? The very next morning, Hoglinda set about making arrangements for the purchase of a harpsichord. Not long afterwards, the instrument was delivered to Quiller's house - accompanied by Hoglinda herself, for a harpsichord without a teacher would have just been frustrating. Thereafter, Hoglinda visited once a week to oversee the hoglets' musical education. Just as she had hoped, her father never questioned this arrangement; and naturally, having come so far, she always stayed the night. This gave her plenty of time to join Quiller, Snipwicke and Spinet when they met at Bristlestone Mill to discuss the latest news.

The long-expected declaration of war between Great Bristlin and Furze came in March and was much discussed. Not so well known was that, shortly before this, a hedgehog by the name of Roundcroft had departed Furze for Great Bristlin. Roundcroft was from the colonies and had been working as a secretary for the rebel diplomats, while they were negotiating their secret treaty with the Furzish. He was also a secret Loyalist and a Bristlish spy. Espinon never discovered his identity. As for the likely success of Espinon's invasion plan, Quiller had already sown the seeds of doubt within the Furzish government. Of course, Espinon was very attached to his plan and did his best to argue in its favour. But, as Quiller's reports continued to come in, suggesting less and less favourable conditions for an invasion, the Furzish government finally said that enough was enough. Hérispionne had assured them Quiller was reliable, and other sources of intelligence only seemed to confirm this. So the invasion was finally abandoned, and the Isle of Needles and its inhabitants were safe.

With the requirement to report to Hérispionne now over, the weekly meetings between Hoglinda, Snipwicke, Quiller and Spinet might easily have come to an end. But such was the bond that had grown between the four hedgehogs and so accustomed had they become to one another's company, that they continued to meet just as before. Naturally, their conversation often turned to smuggling. And, when it did, Hoglinda listened with as much interest as ever - despite her mixed feelings on the subject. Indeed, the temptation to get involved again was too hard to resist. After all, if she could not lend a paw to her friends from time to time, when they were in need, what use was she to anyone?

The very first thing she did was secure the release of poor old Rip and Tar from the navy, having persuaded her father to intercede on their behalf. Though she never admitted her role in their release, Snipwicke and Spinet did not doubt it, and their gratitude was surpassed only by their affection for her. As time went on, Hoglinda also became a regular customer of Mr Snipwicke's, buying such items as tea, gloves and lace for herself, and snuff and brandy for her father. The extra income made all the difference to Mr Snipwicke, who was now able to carry out some long overdue repairs and even improvements to Bristlestone Mill. As a result of this, the mill produced more flour, and at long last Snipwicke's milling business began to turn in a real profit.

As for Quiller, knowing the ropes of his business as she did, Hoglinda gave him advice whenever he sought it. This was increasingly often, for he valued her opinion very highly these days. Now and then, she would become more actively involved in a smuggling run. Mr Tubby was getting on in years and his health was

sometimes poor; on such occasions, Hoglinda would step in and help to organize the shore party for him. Very soon it emerged that she had a talent for organization. And, as her experience grew, so did her reputation and influence among the smugglers on the Back. Sometimes she could even be found on the beach when the *Hogspur* came in, supervising the shore party in place of Mr Tubby. No one questioned her presence there or her authority. It was accepted she was one of them now. Hoglinda, who had once tried to put a stop to Quiller's smuggling, was now a smuggler herself - one of the smugglers of Hog's Head Bay.

POSTSCRIPT: the facts behind the story

There is much about *The Smugglers of Hog's Head Bay* which resembles circumstances and events in our own human world during the years 1777-8. You may therefore be interested to read the following account of smuggling, sailing, war and locations in our late 18th century[1].

Smuggling in 18th Century Britain

Smuggling is bringing goods or people into or out of the country illegally. There are three broad types of smuggling: 1) smuggling to escape paying tax 2) smuggling illegal items and 3) smuggling of people. All smuggling before the 20th century was of the first type.

Smuggling was common in 18th century Britain. Many people were involved in it and many more bought smuggled goods. The goods were ones which were heavily taxed[2]. By not paying tax, smugglers were able to sell their goods much more cheaply than lawful traders and still make a lot of money. The higher taxes rose, the more profitable and the more popular smuggling became.

The Customs Service was responsible for both collecting the tax on imports and catching smugglers. It was a very difficult and dangerous job. They had a huge coastline to guard, and not many men to do it with. Those men seldom knew the coast as well as the smugglers; they were also badly equipped and badly paid; sometimes they even turned a blind eye to smuggling in return for money.

People from all levels and sections of society were involved in smuggling – from fishermen and farm workers to the gentry and clergy. Some of these people could have lived very comfortably without smuggling; but there were many others who lived in extreme poverty. Smugglers may also have been influenced by the fact that very little of the money raised through import taxes was spent on the civilian population: during the late 1770s and the 1780s, around 90% of government spending was on war. Most smugglers were men, but women were involved, too. They played a land-based role, helping to hide, carry and sell contraband. Women were also frequently responsible for the colouring and dilution of brandy, which was

---

[1] The 18th century is the same as the 1700s – just as the 21st century is the 2000s.
[2] E.g. tea, wine, brandy, port, gin, salt, lace, silk, gloves, tobacco and snuff.

necessary to make it drinkable. In a few exceptional cases women even became leaders of smuggling groups.

The methods used by smugglers varied a great deal. Sometimes the contraband was smuggled in right under the Customs' noses. A boat would come into port quite openly, and the tax would be paid on the low-taxed goods carried on board, but the high-taxed goods would be hidden, for example beneath a false bottom. Alternatively, an innocent-looking person on a passenger boat might have lace or silk hidden on his or her person. On a poorly guarded coast, the smugglers usually aimed to bring in their cargo when no one was looking – when "the coast was clear". This was often done under cover of darkness and then preferably on a moonless night. There were other cases, however, where the smugglers were so many and so well armed that they made very little effort to hide their activities but relied upon force instead. If the Customs turned up, they responded with violence.

When the contraband was brought ashore, it had to be hidden. Sometimes it was too risky to carry it away immediately (such as if coming ashore in daylight). It might then be hidden in a cave or bushes or buried on the beach. When it was safe to do so, the smugglers would return and take the contraband inland to be stored. Hiding places were found in lofts, cellars, outbuildings, church towers and tombs; and some houses had specially-built hiding places, like the one in Quiller's house.

Money usually had to be found in advance of a smuggling run, in order to pay for the cargo; but this was not always the case. The smugglers of Polperro in Cornwall did not have to pay for the goods until after they had sold them. This was thanks to a rather extraordinary man called Zephaniah Job, who acted as a banking agent between the Polperro smugglers and the Guernsey merchants from whom the smugglers bought their goods. Because the merchants knew they could trust Job to collect the money on their behalf, they were happy to wait. Job later took a more active role in smuggling, when he and an associate bought a smuggling lugger. This associate was coincidentally called John Quiller. My own Quiller, however, has more in common with Job himself, for he too acts as a banking agent, collecting money from the smugglers and passing it on to the merchants.

Although smuggling took place along almost the entire coastline of Great Britain, it was a particularly serious problem along the south coast of England, including the Isle of Wight. This was because of its being so close to France, the Netherlands and the Channel Islands, where most of the contraband was bought.

The Isle of Wight

Hoglinda's home, the Isle of Needles, bears a striking resemblance to our Isle of Wight as it would have been in the 18th century. Situated just off the south coast of England, this was a place that few mainlanders visited in the 1770s. The south west of the island, often referred to as the Back of the Wight[3], was particularly cut off and remote, thanks to the downs (hills) surrounding it.

The island's most famous natural landmark is the Needles Rocks. The Needles are three tall columns of chalk rising from the sea. There was once a fourth rock in the shape of a needle, called Lot's Wife or Cleopatra's Needle, but this collapsed in 1764[4]. In fact, the geography of the Isle of Wight has undergone quite a few significant changes since the 18th century, which may interest readers living on or visiting the island today. For example, the harbour at Brading (similar to Brambling in the story) no longer exists: an embankment was built in 1881 and the land drained. And the River Yar[5] (my River Hogwash) appears much wider on 18th century maps and prints than it does today.

Hog's Head Bay, at the centre of the story, is very similar to Freshwater Bay, which lies on the south-west coast of the Isle of Wight; and the Hog's Head Inn resembles the Mermaid Inn, which once stood towards the west end of the bay, where the Albion Hotel stands now. In the 18th century, the inn, the bay and its caves were all used by smugglers – although among smugglers the Mermaid was known as "The Cabin". Of the various caves in the bay, the most famous was Freshwater Cave, which was popular with artists from the 1790s. These days you can visit the caves by kayak or (very rarely) on foot. However, it can still be dangerous, as you can easily get cut off by the tide, as Hoglinda was. So you should always consult a local and go with an adult.

Another feature of the island once used by smugglers were its many chines. The chines are deep ravines in the cliffs, formed by streams. They provided an easy well-hidden route off the beach for the

---

[3] Or simply "the Back". It is an area roughly from Freshwater to St Catherine's Point.
[4] Early 17th century charts show a cluster of similar pencil-shaped chalk stacks on the north-west side of the Needles. Clearly Lot's Wife was the last of them.
[5] Sometimes referred to as the Western Yar, as there are two River Yars on the Isle of Wight.

smugglers to carry their contraband away. In the 18th century, they would have been much longer than today. Thanks to coastal erosion and landslips, the island, in some parts of the south coast, loses an average of six feet or two metres a year to the sea. Assuming a constant rate of erosion, that would add up to almost ⅓ mile or ½ kilometre lost to the sea since 1777-8.

For much of the 18th century, the Isle of Wight was only lightly guarded by the Customs Service. In 1777, William Arnold became HM Collector of Customs for the Isle of Wight, based at Cowes on the north coast of the island. In the following years, Arnold worked hard to improve the effectiveness of the Customs Service and had some success. However, his efforts appear to have been focussed chiefly on the Solent (the strait separating the Isle of Wight from the mainland of England). This was where the large smuggling ships were usually to be found, but many of them appear to have been bound for the mainland, rather than the Isle of Wight. Meanwhile, the wild south coast of the island received less attention, and the smugglers there continued to rely chiefly upon secrecy rather than force to run their cargos ashore.

There were no large smuggling gangs on the Isle of Wight, of the type found particularly in Kent and Sussex. Yet smuggling was rife on the island and enjoyed widespread support well into the 19th century. Charles Deane, coastguard commander in 1836, said that "8 out of 10 of the whole population are consumers of contraband spirits, tobacco and tea, and ... they consider ... there is no harm in it." In 1860, poet Sydney Dobell wrote: "The whole population here are smugglers. Everyone has an ostensible occupation, but nobody gets his money by it, or cares to work in it. Here are fishermen who never fish, but always have pockets full of money, and farmers whose farming consists in ploughing the deep by night, and whose daily time is spent in standing like herons on lookout posts."

One such smuggler whose story has come down to us was James Buckett born in 1805 in Brighstone (similar to Bristlestone in the story). Buckett started smuggling in his teens. He and a friend would sail across to France in a 20-foot sailing boat. Weather permitting, they would then return on a moonless night and unload and carry away the tubs before daylight. On their way back, they would keep a look-out for Customs cutters. If they saw anything suspicious, they would drop their tubs into the sea, in the manner described in the story. Eventually, Buckett was caught and sentenced to serve in the Royal Navy for five years.

The Press Gangs

The forcible recruitment of men into the Royal Navy was called impressment. This was a common punishment for smugglers in the 18th century, but you did not have to be convicted of a crime to be impressed. Any seafaring man was liable to be grabbed by the press gangs of the navy's Impress Service. This practice, which was to make up for the shortage of volunteers, was extremely unpopular with the public, and many believed it to be contrary to the British constitution, but it continued until 1815. In the story, Snipwicke's crew are grabbed not because they are smugglers but because they are sailors.

The Channel Islands

The Channel Islands[6] are not part of the United Kingdom but a group of self-governing dependencies of the British Crown. Situated on the far side of the English Channel, they lie close to the French coast; and in the 18th century most islanders spoke French or a local version of Norman French. With their position on the west coast of Europe and their close connections to both France and Great Britain, the islands became important centres of international trade at this time. The most developed port of all in the Channel Islands was St Peter Port, capital of Guernsey. (St Peter Port would then have looked quite similar to St Pricklier Port as portrayed in the story; just as Guernsey has similarities to Gruntsey.)

Though loyal subjects of the British king and dependent upon Great Britain for their defence, the Channel Islanders created their own laws and still do. They could not be taxed by the British government and were free to sell their goods to whomever they wished. Though some merchants preferred not to trade with smugglers, others did not hesitate. Large quantities of cargos were sold openly and legally to both English and French smugglers. This trade reached its height on Guernsey between 1770 and 1820. A secondary industry also flourished on Guernsey as a result: the manufacture of small, easily-carried barrels, of the type specifically used by smugglers. By 1805, there were 600 coopers engaged in making them.

---

[6] The five main islands are Jersey, Guernsey, Alderney, Sark and Herm.

The Huguenots

You may remember that Madame Hérispionne pretended to be from a "Hoguenot" family. In the human world, many religious refugees called Huguenots arrived in Guernsey from France in the late 16th century and then again during the late 17th and early 18th centuries. The Huguenots were Protestants[7], like the Guernsey islanders at this time, but they were persecuted in their native France, which was Catholic. By the 1770s, the active persecution had come to an end. But Protestantism remained unlawful until 1787, and until then life cannot have been comfortable for the few Huguenots who remained in France. In the story, Hérispionne's pretended Protestantism would have made it easier for her to marry a Protestant Gruntsey islander.

The American War of Independence 1775-83

The colonial rebellion referred to in the story bears a strong resemblance to the human conflict known as the American War of Independence or American Revolution, which was fought between Great Britain and the "13 Colonies".

The 13 Colonies were part of a wider group of colonies belonging to Great Britain[8], founded on the Atlantic coast of North America in the 17th and 18th centuries. Lying more than 3,000 miles (5,000 km) from Great Britain, the colonies were at first left pretty much to govern themselves. However, the French and Indian War, fought against France in North America 1754-63, left the British government with significant debts. In 1765 the British government imposed new taxes on the colonies to help pay off those debts. But the colonies protested that Britain had no right to tax them because they had no representatives in the British Parliament. To keep order, the British government sent soldiers to America. This led to confrontation and then war in 1775. On 4 July 1776, the 13 Colonies declared their independence as the United States of America.

---

[7] Protestantism is a form of Christian faith and practice. The Protestants broke away from the Catholic Church in the 16th century.

[8] The 13 Colonies were Connecticut, Delaware, Georgia, Maryland, Massachusetts, New Hampshire, New Jersey, North Carolina, New York, Pennsylvania, Rhode Island, South Carolina and Virginia. Great Britain's other American colonies (Florida, Canada and Caribbean islands) did not rebel.

Reactions in Great Britain varied. There were those who were shocked by and wholly opposed to the American Declaration of Independence, and those who were sympathetic to the complaints of the colonists. Others were more worried about the impact of the war on trade.

Not all Americans sought independence. Those who did were called Patriots. Those who remained loyal to the British crown were called Loyalists[9]. Some Loyalists fought for or even spied for the British side. One such Loyalist was Edward Bancroft, a Massachusetts-born scientist. Bancroft went to Paris in March 1777 and worked for the American Commission there, copying letters and other documents, translating diplomatic letters, arranging for repairs, hiring crews and buying supplies for American ships in French ports. He was also a British spy, paid £1,000 for his services; it is believed that, thanks to him, the British may have seen the secret treaty between France and America (see below) just two days after it was signed.

War with France 1778-83

France saw the American Revolution as an opportunity to weaken Great Britain, which she regarded as a threat to her security. She was also anxious for revenge since losing her own American colonies following her defeat by Britain in the French and Indian War[10]. From 1775, France sent secret supplies of gunpowder and ammunition to the American rebels. The British answered this by authorizing British ships to board and search any foreign ships suspected of carrying arms. In December 1777, secret negotiations began, leading to France's recognition of the United States of America on 6 February 1778, with the signing of a Treaty of Alliance. On 17 March 1778, Great Britain declared war on France.

In 1779 and 1780 respectively, Spain and the Netherlands joined the war against Great Britain. The war was now global, as the nations fought in every part of the world where they were in competition. Most worrying of all for the British, however, was the threat of a French invasion. The war had left Great Britain very vulnerable, drawing away 50,000 of her 60,000 troops to fight abroad. On the Isle

---

[9] Following the British defeat about 65-70,000 Loyalists fled the United States (the total population was about 2.5 million people).
[10] France lost Canada and most of New France to Great Britain.

of Wight, the only effective coastal defence was Sandown Fort, with just 150 men.

In the winter of 1777-8, French politician and soldier Charles François Dumouriez prepared a plan for the invasion of the Isle of Wight. The island was well equipped to maintain an occupying force, and Dumouriez planned to turn it into an island fortress. It had a military hospital, stores of corn and other provisions at Brading and St Helens, and naval construction yards at Cowes. Apart from those needed to work on the farms, the entire population was to be transported to the mainland.

The French invasion fleet was to consist of two hundred oyster-ketches - shallow-draught boats suitable for beaching. They would depart from Cherbourg in France and land 12,000 men (the entire population of the Isle of Wight at this time was only 18,000). The intention was to set sail during the oyster-fishing season in order to provide cover for the invasion, and a date was set for November 1778.

Thirty of the ketches would be converted into gun-boats and, together with some French Navy warships, would occupy Brading Harbour and the coast off Ryde. Soldiers would be landed on the south coast - the main force at Sandown Bay, and others at Chale Bay, Brighstone Bay and Freshwater Bay. To guide the boats safely ashore along the dangerous south coast of the island, pilots were recruited from among English and French smugglers.[11]

Preparations for the invasion were begun. But then the port of departure was changed, Portsmouth was added to the invasion plan and it was decided to use a normal naval force instead of oyster-ketches. Costs rose, the chances of success fell and eventually the plan was abandoned.

The Peace

Peace came in 1783. Great Britain was defeated and recognized the independence of the United States of America. The loss of the 13 Colonies was a shock for many in Britain, the war had been costly and trade had suffered badly. However, by 1785 trade between the two countries was back at pre-war levels and by 1792 it had doubled. Although it may not have seemed like it at the time, American

---

[11] English smugglers would again help France in the Napoleonic Wars (1803-1815). Napoleon said, "They did great mischief to your government. During the war, all the information I received came through smugglers …they took over spies from France."

independence was probably good for Britain as well as for the United States.

Sailing in the 18th Century

Hoglinda's story takes place in the age of sail. These days most sailing boats are pleasure-craft and relatively small; but in the 18th century the sea was full of sailing craft, from small boats setting a single sail to huge warships setting more than thirty sails.

Navigation[12] was much harder in the 18th century than now, with all our digital instruments. The instruments used back then included the log-line to measure speed and the lead-line to measure depth in coastal waters; the lead-line was especially used in foggy or hazy weather.

A **log-line** consisted of a line (rope)[13] which had a knot tied along its length every 47 feet (14.3 metres) and a log (a weighted piece of wood) attached to the end. The log was thrown into the water; as the boat travelled forwards, the line would unravel and the knots were counted off for a period of 28 seconds. The total number of knots counted gave the speed of the boat, which was therefore expressed in "knots", one knot being equal to one nautical mile per hour[14]. In the UK, we still use the word "knots" as the unit of speed at sea today.

The **lead-line** consisted of a line or rope[15] with markers along its length and a lead weight attached to the end. The lead weight was thrown overboard. When it reached the bottom of the sea, a sounding (measurement) was taken by noting the marker closest to the surface of the sea. The markers were traditionally a variety of textures and colours, to make it easy to read them in daylight and at night. The lead-line also showed what type of seabed lay below: a lump of sticky tallow, pressed into a hollow at the base of the weight, would bring up bits of sand or mud etc.; if it came up clean, it meant rock below.

The Moon and the stars were also used for navigation; but, when it came to running contraband ashore, smugglers preferred to do so in **"the darks"** i.e. three days either side of a New Moon. The New Moon is when the Moon's surface appears dark to us because the side of the Moon that is lit by the Sun is facing away from the Earth. As the Moon orbits the Earth over a period of 29.5 days, our view of it changes. We

---

[12] The act of finding your way from one place to another, especially at sea.
[13] 150 fathoms or 900 feet or 274 metres long.
[14] 1 nautical mile per hour is the same as 1.15 (land) miles per hour or 1.85 kilometres per hour.
[15] Usually 25 fathoms long (150 feet or 46 metres).

see it grow from a thin crescent to a Full Moon (when the lit half of the Moon is facing us) and then shrink back down to a New Moon again.

The Moon is also largely responsible for **tidal movement** - the rising and falling of the sea which occurs throughout the day. For sailing ships in the 18th century and now, an understanding of tides and tidal currents was very important both for navigation and for deciding a time of departure.

In the UK, we usually have two high tides and two low tides a day. This tidal movement is caused by the Moon's gravity. On the side of the Earth closest to the Moon, the water is pulled away from the seabed, resulting in a high tide. On the side of the Earth furthest away from the Moon, the seabed is pulled away from the water, also resulting in a high tide. In between are the low tides.

Spring tides[16] occur when the Moon, the Earth *and* the Sun are aligned[17], which is roughly once a fortnight, when there is a New Moon or Full Moon: this results in extremes of high and low tide. In between this, are the neap tides, when high and low tide are more moderate. **See the diagram opposite.**

The tides are also influenced by other things, such as sea currents, winds, the shape of the sea floor and the shore. All of this makes it very difficult to predict the tide times in any one spot (as Hoglinda finds out to her cost!); so you should always check the tide times online[18] if there is any chance of your being cut off.

---

[16] So called because the sea springs up.
[17] The effect of the Sun is less than that of the Moon because it is farther away.
[18] www.ukho.gov.uk/Easytide.

Moon Phases and their Effect upon Tides

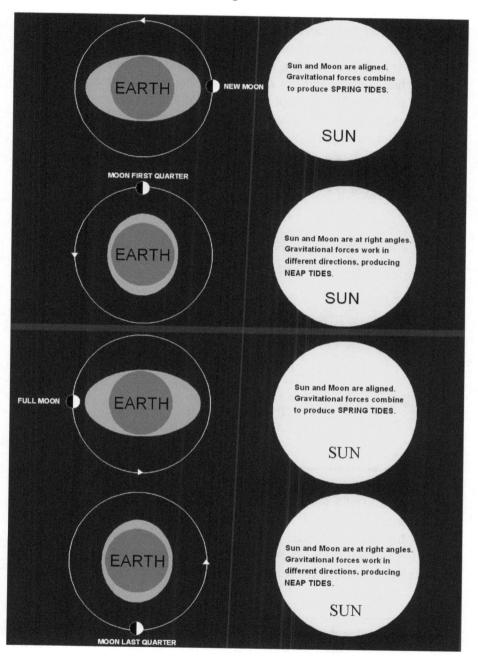

Customs' and Smugglers' Boats and Ships[19]

The Customs Service employed small ships called cutters, which were built for speed: the name "cutter" may refer to "cutting" through the water quickly. A **cutter** in those days was defined as having at least two headsails, usually a single mast, and a running bowsprit (see **diagram below**). The bowsprit allowed for a greater area of sail; and being "running" meant it could be taken off and stored in the boat in rough weather or in port.

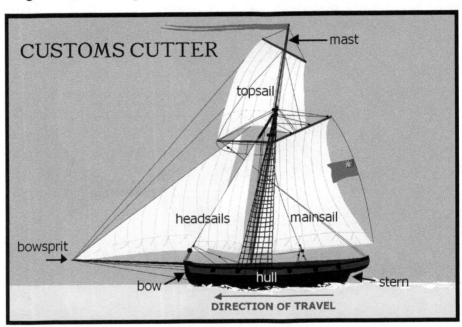

Smugglers used a greater variety of boat types, including cutters but also rowing boats[20] and luggers small and large, as featured in the story. A **lugger** is any boat or ship whose principal sail is a lugsail - a four-sided sail whose head is shorter than its foot and whose luff (front edge) is shorter than its leech (back edge). The lugsail comes in a

---

[19] There is no absolute difference between a ship and a boat. But, generally speaking, a ship is larger than a boat, and a boat can be carried on a ship but not the other way around! In the story, the *Sea Urchin* is always referred to as a boat; the *Hogspur* and the Customs cutter are generally referred to as ships, but they are small ships.

[20] Many Isle of Wight smugglers seem to have crossed the Channel in rowing boats!

variety of forms, including the dipping and standing lugsails featured in the story (**see diagrams on the next page**).

When sailing across the wind, a dipping lugsail is moved to the other side of the mast by dipping its head and pulling it around, as Spinet is shown doing on page 126. A standing lugsail always remains on the same side of the mast (wherever the wind is coming from, which may look very odd to those sailors among you!): this makes the sail less efficient but very easy to handle. Luggers were very popular in the late 18th century, being simple, robust and efficient[21]. They had one to three masts.

---

[21] The lugger is more powerful in relation to the size of the hull and better at sailing to windward than other traditional rigs.

Diagrams below – the *Sea Urchin's* mainsail and the *Hogspur's* foresail are dipping lugsails. The *Sea Urchin's* mizzensail and the *Hogspur's* mainsail and mizzensail are standing lugsails.

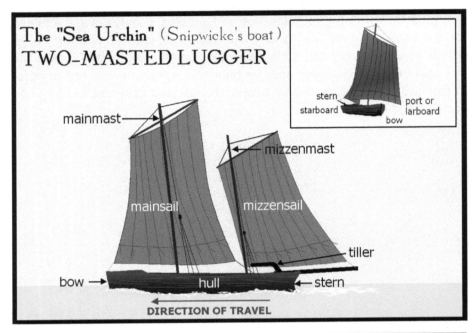

The "Sea Urchin" (Snipwicke's boat)
TWO-MASTED LUGGER

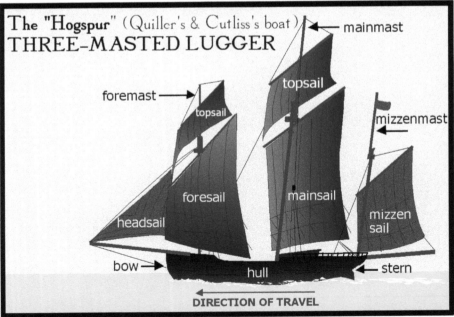

The "Hogspur" (Quiller's & Cutliss's boat)
THREE-MASTED LUGGER

174

Select Bibliography

A Dictionary of the Isle of Wight Dialect, and Provincialisms Used, by William Henry Long

A Short History of Guernsey, by Peter Johnston

At War with the Smugglers, by Rear-Admiral D. Arnold-Forster

Sailing Rigs, An Illustrated Guide, by Jenny Bennett

Smugglers of the Isle of Wight, by Richard J. Hutchings

Smuggling in the British Isles, by Richard Platt

Smuggling on Wight Island, by R.F. Dowling

The Guernsey Merchants and their world, by Gregory Stevens Cox

The Isle of Wight, An Illustrated History, by Jack and Johanna Jones

The Smugglers' Banker, The Story of Zephaniah Job of Polperro, by Jeremy Rowett Johns

Wight Hazards, by Peter Bruce

Glossary

This is an explanation of some of the vocabulary as used in the story. Words marked "nautical" relate to boats, sailing and the sea. Some words have additional meanings, which are not explained here. The Isle of Wight dialect is no longer heard, though some words survive in other forms of English.

adrift *(nautical)*	With no means of controlling your boat (e.g. oars, sails) and therefore at the mercy of the wind and tide. Used metaphorically, "casting yourself adrift" means separating yourself from someone or something.
afore	Before (used in Isle of Wight dialect).
all at sea *(nautical metaphor)*	In a state of confusion and uncertainty. The expression refers to a sailor out of sight of land and lost.
allies	People or countries that help each other.
anker	A unit of measurement equal to 10 gallons or 45 litres. Half-anker barrels were used by smugglers because they were relatively light and easy to carry. They were often strapped one at the front and one at the back, as depicted on the front cover. Traders who had nothing to hide used much larger containers.
auberge	French word for an inn (pub offering food and beds).
authorities	Organization with official powers.
axed	Asked (used in Isle of Wight dialect).
Back (of the Wight)	The south-west part of the Isle of Wight, roughly between Freshwater and St Catherine's Point.
barrel	A type of container.
beached *(nautical)*	Brought up onto the beach out of the water.
to **bear away** *(nautical)*	To turn a vessel away from the wind.

to **take a bearing** (*nautical*)	To work out your location at sea with the aid of landmarks. Using a compass, draw a line on a chart from a landmark, e.g. a lighthouse, towards your boat. Repeat with a second landmark. Your boat is where the lines meet. Experienced sailors who can judge distance are usually able to manage, in practice, with one landmark.
to **beat to windward** (*nautical*)	It is impossible to sail directly into the wind, so a sailor wanting to travel to windward will instead "beat to windward" i.e. zigzag as close into the wind as possible.
berth (*nautical*)	A sleeping place on a ship.
between the devil and the deep blue sea (*metaphor*)	In a difficult situation where there are two equally unpleasant choices.
bist	Are (2nd person singular – used in Isle of Wight dialect).
bow	Front of a ship or boat.
to **burn your boats** (*nautical metaphor*)	To cut yourself off from any chance of going back or returning to how things were before.
capital (*money*)	Wealth owned by a person / organization.
capsize (*nautical*)	To overturn in the water.
cargo (*nautical*)	Goods carried on a ship or boat.
casn't	Can't (used in Isle of Wight dialect).
casualties	People killed or injured in an accident or battle.
chine	Ravine in a cliff formed by a stream. A term used in the Isle of Wight, Hampshire, Dorset and Devon.
close-hauled (*nautical*)	Sailing close to the wind, with the sails pulled in tight.
the **coast is clear** (*nautical*)	An expression used when attempting a landing from sea in enemy territory, meaning the coast is clear of enemies. Also used metaphorically to mean there is no danger of being observed or caught.

colony	A country or area under the political control of another country and occupied by settlers from that country.
compatriot	A person from the same country.
contraband	Smuggled goods.
cooper	Maker or repairer of barrels.
course *(nautical)*	Direction of travel. To "set a course" on a sailing vessel is to set your sails so as to travel in a particular direction.
crew *(nautical)*	The people who sail or work on a ship or boat.
Crimany!	Exclamation of surprise and displeasure (used in Isle of Wight dialect).
Customs	The Customs Service was the organization responsible for collecting taxes on imported goods and preventing smuggling. Also referred to as the "Preventives".
to **cut and run** *(nautical)*	The surest way of making a quick getaway in a sailing vessel was to **cut** the anchor rope **and run** before the wind. This meant losing the anchor but it was a small price to pay for avoiding capture etc. Used metaphorically, it means to depart hastily, as soon as things start to go wrong.
cutter *(nautical)*	Type of ship. See Postscript & diagram, page 172.
Darn it!	Exclamation of displeasure (used in Isle of Wight dialect).
to **disembark** *(nautical)*	To leave a ship.
downs	Gently rolling hills (used mostly in southern England).
dozen	Twelve.
draught *(nautical)*	Depth of water needed to float a particular boat or ship.
drownen' in thee cups	Drunk (Isle of Wight dialect).
embellish	To add extra details to a story.
esplanade	Long, open and flat area beside the sea, along which people walk for pleasure.

exile	Not being allowed in your own country.
fathom *(nautical)*	A measure of depth in the imperial system, equal to 6 feet or 1.8 metres deep. Origin: the arm span of the average man.
to **fathom something** *(nautical metaphor)*	To come to understand something after much <u>deep</u> thought. Derives from "fathom" as a measure of depth.
fleet *(nautical)*	A group of ships or boats sailing together.
fluent / fluency	Able to / Ability to speak and write easily and accurately, especially in a foreign language.
gangplank *(nautical)*	Movable plank used to board or disembark from a boat.
goods	Things for sale.
governess	Woman employed to teach children in a private household (old-fashioned).
grappling hook	Tool with iron claws, attached to a rope and used for grabbing hold of and/or dragging something.
harbour	A place on the coast where boats shelter.
harpsichord	Piano-like instrument, in which the strings are plucked rather than hit.
to **haul in the sheets** *(nautical)*	To pull tight the sheets (ropes controlling the sails).
headland	Narrow piece of land sticking out to sea.
high and dry *(nautical)*	A boat left "high and dry" has been left sitting on the mud, after the tide has gone out. Used metaphorically: to be in a difficult situation and helpless.
high water / high tide *(nautical)*	Highest level of the tide. See Postscript, pages 170-1.
"Hoguenot"	A **Huguenot** is a French Protestant. See Postscript pages 166.
to **hoist**	To raise using ropes and pulleys.
hull *(nautical)*	The body of a boat or ship. See diagram, page 174.
income	Money received, especially regularly such as through work.

inn	Pub providing food and beds.
investment	Money put into a business in order to make more money.
journal	Old-fashioned word for diary.
to **keel over** *(nautical metaphor)*	To fall over suddenly. (If a boat "keels over", it turns so far onto its side that it cannot recover.)
knots *(nautical)*	A measure of speed, which is still used. One knot equals one nautical mile per hour; a nautical mile is equal to 1.15 (land) miles and 1.85 km.
larboard *(nautical)*	Left side of a boat, when facing forwards. Changed to "port" in 1844, to avoid confusion with "starboard".
late wife	A late wife (or husband or friend etc.) is one who has died.
Le Sieur	A title (e.g. like "Mr") used on Guernsey.
lead-line *(nautical)*	Equipment for measuring depth at sea. See Postscript, page 169.
ledge *(nautical)*	Underwater ridge, especially one of rocks near the shore.
ledger	Book recording money received and paid.
leeway *(nautical)*	The lee of a boat or ship is the side away from the wind. A boat's leeway is the distance she is blown sideways from her intended route. Used metaphorically, leeway describes the measure of freedom to act / move away from the original plan.
line *(nautical)*	Rope on a ship or boat.
log-line *(nautical)*	Equipment for measuring speed at sea. See Postscript, page 169.
loose end/s *(nautical metaphor)*	**"Loose ends"** to be tied up are things still to be completed or explained. The expression refers to the ends of ropes on board a ship: sailors had to tie up any loose ends before they could set sail. To be **"at a loose end"** is to be bored because you have nothing to do: sailors with nothing else to do would be told to check that no ropes had come loose.

low water / low tide *(nautical)*	Lowest level of the tide. See Postscript, pages 170-1.
to **luff up** *(nautical)*	to steer nearer the wind.
lugger *(nautical)*	Type of boat / ship. See Postscript, pages 172-3, and diagram, page 174.
mainmast *(nautical)*	The main mast. See diagram, page 174.
mainsail *(nautical)*	The main sail. This describes the sail in terms of its position, which is on the mainmast. The mainsail can be of many different types. See diagram, page 174.
manoeuvre	A movement or series of movements.
merchant	Person involved in trade on a large scale.
mile	Unit of measurement, still used in the UK and USA. A nautical mile is equal to 1.15 (land) miles and 1.85 km. A land mile is equal to 1.6 km and 0.86 nautical miles.
mill	Building where grain is ground into flour.
mizzenmast *(nautical)*	Mast behind the mainmast. See diagram, page 174.
mizzensail *(nautical)*	This describes the sail in terms of its position, which is on the mizzenmast. It can come in many different forms. See diagram, page 174.
to **moor** *(nautical)*	To attach a boat to an anchor or the shore with a rope.
musket	A type of gun used in the 18th century.
nautical	Concerning sea, sailors, boats or navigation.
"under no **obligation**"	Not required to do something, either morally or legally.
overboard *(nautical)*	Into the water from a boat or ship. Used metaphorically, "to go overboard" means to go too far.
parlour	Old-fashioned word for sitting room.
pauper	Old-fashioned word for very poor person.
"**paw-to-mouth**"	Living "**hand-to-mouth**" means having barely enough money to survive.
persecuted	Treated very badly.
physician	Old-fashioned word for a doctor.

pilot *(nautical)*	Person with expert local knowledge hired to take charge of a ship or boat approaching or leaving the shore.
pin money	Woman's allowance for buying personal items, such as clothes (old-fashioned).
Preventives	Term sometimes used in the 18th and 19th centuries to refer to Customs officials (see Customs).
profit	You make a profit if you get more money out of a business than you put into it.
promissory letter	Signed letter promising to pay a stated sum of money to a particular person.
provisions	Supplies of food, drink or equipment.
prying	Trying to find out something that is none of your business.
quayside	Platform for loading and unloading ships, and the area around it.
recess	A small hollow.
rector	Priest in certain Church of England parishes.
reefed *(nautical)*	To reduce the area of sail exposed to the wind, usually in bad weather or to slow the vessel. To **"shake out the reefs"** is to unreef the sails.
to know / learn / show the **ropes** *(nautical metaphor)*	To know the ropes is to be thoroughly familiar with what needs to be done. An expression of nautical origin arising from the complexity and importance of ropes on board a boat or ship.
to **run before the wind** *(nautical)*	To sail with the wind coming from behind.
sandglass	Device for measuring time. Sand flows from a upper to a lower glass bulb.
scruples	Feelings of doubt over whether an action is morally right.
scuttle *(nautical)*	To sink a vessel on purpose.
to **set sail** *(nautical)*	To begin a sea journey.
sheet *(nautical)*	A rope controlling a sail.
to **sheet in the sails** *(nautical)*	To pull in or tighten the sheets (see above) until the sails stop flapping.

182

shilling	Until decimalization in 1971, a pound was divided into twenty shillings, worth 12 pence each. So there were 240 pence in a pound.
shingle	Small round pebbles on a beach.
skipper *(nautical)*	Informal title for the master or captain of a boat or ship.
somewhen	At some time or other (used in Isle of Wight dialect).
sounding	To **"take a sounding"** is to measure the depth of the sea.
spinet	A small harpsichord (see harpsichord).
spring tide	Very high and low tides which occur at the time of a New or Full Moon.
squeamish	Morally fussy or easily disgusted.
stand by *(nautical)*	Get ready.
starboard *(nautical)*	Right-hand side of a boat or ship when facing forwards.
stem to stern *(nautical)*	From end to end.
stern *(nautical)*	Back of a boat or ship.
steward	Old-fashioned word for a person employed to look after another's property.
strait *(nautical)*	Narrower passage of water linking two larger areas of water.
subjects	People ruled by a king or queen.
summat	Something (used in Isle of Wight dialect).
to **tack** *(nautical)*	To change direction by turning a boat through the wind.
on the wrong **tack** *(nautical metaphor)*	Following the wrong line of argument or course of action.
tail between your legs	Feeling defeated and ashamed.
taken aback *(nautical metaphor)*	To be astounded by something and unable to respond for a moment. The expression comes from when a square-rigged sailing ship was caught by a powerful gust of head wind, which pushed its sails back.
tax	Money collected from people by the government.

'tedden't	It isn't (used in Isle of Wight dialect).
three sheets to the wind *(nautical metaphor)*	Very drunk. Of nautical origin: on a sea vessel, the sheets are the ropes which hold the sails in place. When a sheet comes loose, the sail flaps in the wind.
tides	The rising and falling of the sea. See Postscript, pages 170-1.
tiller *(nautical)*	Horizontal bar used to steer a boat.
tourniquet	Tight bandage to stop bleeding.
trade	The business of buying and selling.
The Trade	Smugglers' term for smuggling.
traitor	Person who betrays his or her country etc.
treachery	Betrayal / going against your country etc.
in a trice	Very quickly (used in Isle of Wight dialect).
tub	Small barrel (in 18th / 19th century usage).
to undercut	To sell goods for less than someone else.
to unfurl *(nautical)*	To unroll (a sail).
unspecified	Not stated.
venture	A risky or daring project.
vessel *(nautical)*	Boat or ship.
vineyard	Land planted with grapes for wine-making.
to vouch for someone	To promise that someone is reliable.
to take the wind out of someone's sails *(nautical)*	Used metaphorically: To make someone feel less confident by saying something they were not expecting. Used literally: to sail to windward of another boat and steal its wind.
widower	Man whose wife has died.

Also by Elizabeth Morley

Where Hedgehogs Dare

Where Hedgehogs Dare takes us forward to 1940 and the Second World War. Hoglinda's great-great-great granddaughter Snippette is about to face the greatest challenge of her life.

Great Bristlin stands alone against Hegemony and needs every hedgehog it can get: Spike has joined His Majesty's Air Force and is flying reconnaissance missions; Clou has formed an escape line to help Bristlish prisoners-of-war on the run. Snippette is now determined to escape from enemy-occupied Gruntsey and do her bit for the war, too, even if it's just making widgets in a factory. However, the mysterious Field Liaison and Espionage Agency (known to its agents as F.L.E.A.) has something altogether more dangerous in mind, and Snippette will soon hold the fate of nations in her paws.

..."*Are you afraid to die?*" *asked the brigadier suddenly.*
Snippette thought for a moment. "Yes, sir."
"Then what the blazes makes you think you could work for an organization like F.L.E.A.?"
"Some things are more important than my fear of dying."...

Where Hedgehogs Dare takes Snippette, Flight Lieutenant Spike and Clou, the Comte de Grif, on a dangerous journey through enemy-occupied territory – a parachute drop, crash landing, secret messages, deception and self-sacrifice. Some will be captured. All risk their lives.

...Spike swerved away from the oncoming planes but then others appeared, as if from nowhere. Suddenly they were on his tail...

..."They know what Clou gets up to... if they do capture him, he'll be shot."...

Also by Elizabeth Morley

Let Sleeping Hedgehogs Spy

Let Sleeping Hedgehogs Spy brings us forward to the present day. Snippette's great-grandson Snipper is looking forward to a skiing holiday away from it all with his friends; but a sinister plot is afoot and their holiday is soon disrupted when he finds himself pitted against a criminal mastermind known only as "Mr E".

Snipper is soon on Mr E's tail. But, along the way, he must protect his friends, hide his identity and decide once and for all whether the hedgehog in blue is friend or foe. Perhaps she is nothing to do with Mr E – perhaps she is just a stranger whose book he had picked up for her – but a book may contain a code or a secret message.

...Snipper opened his eyes and blinked in the glare of her torch.

She pointed it away from him so he could see who it was. He blinked again.

"You!" he snarled.

"You're alive!" she exclaimed.

"Do I disappoint you?" he asked bitterly, staring down the barrel of her gun...

Snipper's journey takes him from the beautiful but dangerous snow-covered slopes of the Altispine Mountains; through the Needlelands where Van Hogloot – a criminal banker with international connections – has his home in a converted windmill; to Icepeak, a remote and starkly beautiful island where Snipper finally comes face-to-face with the mysterious Mr E himself.

...Their eyes met.

"There will be casualties," said Mr E with a sigh, as though it troubled him a little.

It sent a shiver down Snipper's spines...

Also by Elizabeth Morley

Hedgehogs From Outer Space

Hedgehogs from Outer Space is Snipper's second adventure. As the story opens, Snipper is looking forward to watching the launch of the space shuttle. Riding inside will be his friends, Pawline and Schnüffel - astronauts who are to spend the next six months orbiting Earth on board the international space station.

But Snipper never makes it to their launch.

..."We may look similar," said the stranger, "but, if you test my DNA, you'll find appearances can be deceptive."

"You?" said Snipper, suppressing an urge to smile. "From outer space?"...

Whisked off to a distant galaxy, Snipper soon has other things on his mind – a rescue mission, a plot which threatens the future of his entire planet and a seemingly impossible journey home. As he navigates his way across a hostile universe, he must learn to land a spacecraft, assume an alien identity and secretly visit strange new worlds - where days are longer than years and plants survive only underground.

...When the warmth returned to the spaceship, Snipper was in the simulator, stabilizing a virtual wormhole. He knew what it meant. The crew were coming out of hibernation. Wiping the simulator's memory he propelled himself towards the door...

Snipper's friends have long since given him up for lost, but their paths will cross again and then they must all play their part. The future of the Earth rests in their paws.